Janet taught drama and English in comprehensive schools for thirty-five years. During this time, she wrote plays for the pupils to perform and was involved in amateur drama, both as an actor and a director. She has always been an avid reader and her love of literature and a desire to write encouraged her to join a writer's group when she retired. This led to writing short stories and then to writing her first novella, *Charitable Thoughts*. Janet has two children, Kate and Mark, who both have left the nest, and she lives in Brentwood with her husband, Keith.

I would like to dedicate this book to my husband, Keith, my children, Kate and Mark, and my mum.

Janet Howson

CHARITABLE THOUGHTS

AUSTIN MACAULEY PUBLISHERS™

LONDON • CAMBRIDGE • NEW YORK • SHARJAH

A CIP catalogue record for this title is available from the British Library.

ISBN 9781528911306 (Paperback)
ISBN 9781528946803 (ePub e-book)

www.austinmacauley.com

First Published (2020)
Austin Macauley Publishers Ltd
25 Canada Square
Canary Wharf
London
E14 5LQ

I want to acknowledge the numerous charity shops that supplied me with incredible stories. I hope you approve of the way I have used them in *Charitable Thoughts*. I would also like to thank Dawn Knox and Francis Clamp from the Brentwood Writers' Circle, both of whom read my manuscript and offered valuable and constructive advice.

Chapter 1

Brenda woke to an eerie silence; one she could never get used to. This feeling of isolation and loneliness she was experiencing daily since she had retired. Then her mother had died, leaving an aching gap in her life. Today she was going to do something about it.

She had seen a poster in the window of the Charity Shop on the High Street. 'Volunteers required. Full or part time. Please apply within'. So, she had taken the initiative, walked in and put her name down with one of the members of staff and today she would be having her 'Induction Day' with the manager.

She had always loved wandering around the charity shops and tended to make a beeline for them after she had been to the bank or completed her food shop.

Brenda looked at herself in the long hall mirror. She had been puzzled on what to wear and decided on a comfortable outfit. *Comfortable*, she liked that word. It reminded her of being a child and listening to stories on the radio. "Are you sitting comfortably? Then we shall begin."

Or her mother's words to her as they left the house, "Make yourself comfortable," to avoid the inevitable toilet stops that may occur otherwise.

In the end, she had settled on a blue skirt, white blouse and a blue cardigan with sensible brogues that were kind to her bunion. She had got rid of all her suits when she retired, pushing them into black bin liners and taking them to the very Charity Shop she was now volunteering in.

She had never got on with the young girls in the office with their teetering, high heels, long nails and short skirts, laughing behind her back at her 'dowdy' appearance and old-fashioned views.

Brenda sighed, adjusted her skirt and donned her thick 'duvet' coat, as she nicknamed it. It would be a protection against the cold winter weather and sharp wind. She remembered her folding umbrella at the last minute. *The sky looks threatening,* she thought to herself, *I might be glad of it later.*

She had decided to walk. The shop shut at 4:30 p.m. but she might be required to tidy up, sweep around or wash up the teacups – she presumed there would be a cup of tea sometime during the afternoon? It would be far too long to leave her car in a carpark. She objected to paying for a carpark ticket. Once, she had been three minutes late returning to pick up her car and was horrified to discover a yellow bag on the front windscreen announcing the parking penalty. The walk normally took her twenty minutes into the centre of town. The Charity Shop was favourably placed being next to the main shops in the High Street.

When she arrived at the shop, a wave of nerves hit her. She almost turned back. However, she took a deep breath and entered. There were a few customers sorting through the handrails and an elderly man standing behind the till, endeavouring with obvious difficulty to keep his eyes open. He was dressed smartly in a suit and tie; his grey hair was tidy and he was well-shaven. She assumed he was the morning shift. She also spotted a lady with her back to her, sorting out the DVDs. She thought it would be wisest to approach the morning shift, so, donning a smile, she approached the till.

"Hello, I am Brenda Watts, I'm here for my Induction Day. The manager, George Forbes, said he would be going through everything with me. Do you know where I could find him?"

The man at the till was now wide-awake, eyeing her suspiciously. After a moment, he seemed to get a grip of the situation. "Wait here…" He was about to leave his sentry post by the till when something made him stop. "Can't leave the shop floor. Things get nicked, you'd be surprised how much stuff gets nicked. You wouldn't think people would be so callous as to steal from a charity shop."

He pulled out a rather grimy handkerchief and blew his nose loudly. "Once they have exhausted our shop, they are on to the next. Nothing better to do. I once suggested to one lady who had been in the shop over an hour that she become a volunteer. I might as well have suggested she abseiled down the side of the Shard!" he chuckled at his own joke.

She wondered how long he would carry on with his rather off-putting tales when George Forbes appeared from the back of the shop. He was wearing jeans that were too big for him and a sweatshirt that had seen better days. He looked in a rush and rather anxious. On seeing her, he weaved his way to the till through the customers. She put on her smile that she thought looked confident. There was an awkward moment when she thought he was going to shake her hand and brought hers up to meet his. However, he was merely scratching his head, a habit she would witness repeating itself during the afternoon. Embarrassed, she put her arm down by her side.

"It's Brenda, isn't it? So glad you could make it. We only spoke briefly the other day when you popped in. We have been very short of staff today but I am sure Alan is very capable of holding the fort whilst we go out the back for the induction talk, aren't you, Alan?" Alan looked anything but, in fact, she thought, she would be surprised if Alan was still awake on their return. She found herself following George. Dodging around the customers, they ended up in a room filled with boxes, clothes rails towering piles of books and general organised chaos.

"Let's sit here and go through 'Health and Safety' and 'Accident Prevention Strategies'." It was obvious he had repeated these ad nauseum and the words tripped off his tongue without the necessity of looking at a pamphlet or brochure. It was all common sense to her and she gradually began to feel less apprehensive, allowing herself to relax a bit. She interjected with the odd 'yes' and 'I see' or 'I can manage that' in the appropriate places. He sprung up at one point, like a jack in a box, returning with a pair of white rubber gloves. "These are to sort through the clothes with," he explained, "you would be horrified at the amount of dirty clothing we receive, even underwear." She inwardly recoiled at this, although it did not really surprise her at all. Some people's standards were very low.

He had jumped up again, returning this time with a gun, not the firearm type. She smiled to herself at the thought of that. This was a clothes-labelling gun that thrust a spike through each item affixing a price tag to it. He demonstrated on a dress that had obviously been spiked on numerous occasions to explain the technique to new recruits. Well, that all seemed fairly simple. She was allowed to have a few trail spikes and eventually mastered the task, handing the gun back to George, who again was scratching his head, triumphantly.

Once again, she saw him catapulting from his seat, returning with a curious object that she did not recognise. "The steam wand," he explained, "we hang up the suits, dresses, skirts and trousers and steam the creases out. A wonderful invention, saves all that tedious ironing." She attempted to put an expression of being truly impressed on her face. Well, perhaps she was, just a little bit.

Having finished the backroom induction talk, he guided her back to the shop floor and showed her how the clothing was hung on the rails, sized and grouped into colour ranges. She liked that. She appreciated order. She felt it was all straightforward and was about to say so when she realised George had made a beeline for the till. She quickly followed him. Here he went into intricate detail, with accompanying head scratches, about the Gift Aid, Pink Stickers, World Cancer Day, stand up to Cancer Day and finally, with apologetic tones, introduced the topic of 'shaking the bucket'. This was a periodic stint of standing with a tin in the High Street, collecting donations from often reluctant, over-busy pedestrians who had not quite perfected the ability to avoid eye contact. "It can be quite cold," he explained, "so we don't ask you to do it often," he quickly added.

"Would you like to start on the till or in the store room?" George had obviously finished the induction.

"The till, please," she replied, "If you think I'd manage all right?"

"You won't know 'till' you try!" he roared with laughter at his own joke. She responded as well as she could with a short chuckle, but her mind was already on the daunting task of being in sole charge of the incoming money. Alan had disappeared – she assumed he had completed his shift and she couldn't see any sign of the lady who had been filling shelves.

"Break a leg," shouted George as she watched his retreating back disappear into the stockroom. It wasn't until then that she realised that she still had her coat on and her handbag was on her arm. Too embarrassed to call George back she put them both under the counter. *Needs must,* she thought to herself.

Then she waited. She wondered how long it would be before she could test out her newly acquired shop skills. There were six people altogether, roaming around, picking up pieces of memorabilia, reading the first chapter of a book, sifting through the CD and DVD rack, holding up clothes to the light or against their body for size. No movement towards the till though.

"Excuse me," she was shaken out of her reverie by a voice that seemed to come from nowhere. She then realised it was a child of about five years old whose head hardly rose above the height of the counter. "I want this," the voice continued.

She leaned over and extracted a large, fluffy rabbit from the hands of the infant purchaser and was about to look at the price label attached to said animal's ear when a much larger hand extracted it from her grip, removing the infant simultaneously. "She don't want that, little so and so. She can't keep her hands off anything. She's got too many toys as it is, 'er dad spoils 'er rotten." With that she strode out of the shop, steering a now grizzling child in front of her.

She felt quite deflated. Her first sale and it turned out not to be a sale. Still, she put that down to beginner's bad luck. "How much?" A strident woman, with a voice to match, was standing at the counter. She pulled herself together. She examined the black gloves as the customer rummaged through her purse. She realised there was no price tag on them. Thinking on her feet she calculated how much the gloves would be worth. "£2.50 please. Is that okay?" she ventured.

"Those are my bleeding gloves; this is what I am buying." The customer pushed a set of soaps in a box towards her from the place it had been positioned; Brenda excused herself with the fact that it was further away than the gloves, but it didn't make her feel any less stupid.

"Do you need a bag?" she asked.

"You flaming charge for them now, don't you? A bleeding disgrace, if you ask me. No, I'll stick 'em in me bag." At which she did exactly that, paid the required £1.50 and disappeared out of the shop.

She thought about this, *One no sale and one sale, eventually happening after her initial mistake. Not a brilliant record up to now. It could only get better surely.*

She checked her watch. 3:35 p.m., just under an hour to closing. Still no offer of a cup of tea. She was just weighing up the pros and cons of trying to locate George when a group of secondary school pupils pushed through the shop door and descended on the handbags.

"This all you've got?" one of them shouted across to her through a mouth of chewing gum, repositioning her school bag on her back.

She panicked. She didn't know if they had any more handbags or not. She would have to call for George.

"What is it you are looking for?"

"Don't know till I see 'em, do I?"

She considered this for a moment. "I will ask if we have anything out the back. Won't be long." She hurried into the storeroom and called George. He hurried out at a pace appropriate to responding to a fire alarm.

"What is it? Is there something wrong?" His head scratching became quite manic. He seemed a bit irritable, which she thought was rather unfair, as it was her first day.

She explained the situation to him. He eyed up the group of girls. "Only what you see on the shelves. We haven't priced and labelled the rest yet."

"Load of rubbish if you ask me," one of the girls exclaimed as she tossed a bag she was examining back on the pile. "Get one cheaper at Primark."

"Could I suggest you take your loud voices and rude remarks and go to Primark then!" She couldn't believe she had said it. Perhaps it was the tensions of the whole day getting the better of her. She blushed, not knowing quite what to do. Apologise?

"Oh, charming!" this came from the gum chewer.

"Oh, come on, Sophie. Silly cow can 'do one'!" one of the others shouted.

"We ain't coming in here again, smells of sweaty trainers anyway!" one of the others joined in. At that, they all left the shop as loudly as they had entered it.

Quite what 'do one' meant she wasn't really sure and did not really want to find out. More important was the fact that George had been witness to her being dismissive of potential customers. This was her third failure on her first day. She felt quite despondent. She turned around, expecting George to be scowling at the least, instead he was beaming from ear to ear.

"I've wanted to say something similar to those girls for months. They come in here about three times a week, demanding we go out the back to look for an item and disappear, probably with a good selection of the stock. I've never been able to catch them and I've never confronted them. Well done, hopefully, that is the last we'll see of them," he paused, savouring the thought, "now how about I make you a nice cup of tea and you make yourself comfortable in the back room for ten minutes whilst you drink it. I'll lock the doors and get ready to go. My bus is in twenty minutes but we've time for a quick chat."

Comfortable…she smiled at the use of her favourite word. So, feeling quite proud of herself that she had triumphed over the rude girls, she bent down to retrieve her handbag from under the counter. The handbag wasn't there. She searched again, with a sinking heart and a deflated self-esteem.

Oh well, she thought, *those girls did find a handbag to suit them after all.*

Chapter 2

When had they managed to find the bag and then get it out of the shop? Brenda ruminated, then she remembered she had gone to the storeroom to find George hence leaving the shop floor. Why hadn't she remembered what Alan had said about his inability to leave the till unguarded. She could kick herself.

Then she pulled herself up. She shouldn't really be making assumptions that it was definitely the schoolgirls who took the bag. She weighed up the evidence. They had come into the shop specifically looking for a handbag. They had maintained there was nothing in the shop they liked, prompting Brenda to suggest the storeroom. She couldn't imagine it was the little girl who had been frog marched off by her mother or the woman who bought the soaps. No, it must have been the school girls. She called out to George who had mumbled about checking the fire doors and putting on the alarm. After a minute or two, he returned, already wrapped in what could only be described as large child's duffle coat. Brenda wondered if he had purchased it from the shop. On his head was a woolly bobble hat with West Ham written on it and he had donned a pair of patterned wellingtons. The effect was rather disturbing. He reminded her of a toy Paddington Bear that had been discarded by a child and destined to be left in a corner, forgotten and unloved. She pushed the image from her mind. George had obviously been at the back of the queue when they were handing out sartorial elegance.

"George, I am so sorry to trouble you, but my handbag has gone." As the sentence left her lips, she grew cold. Her door keys! She wouldn't be able to get into her flat! The thought astounded her. What was she going to do? Her car keys were on the same chain. The whole enormity of the situation hit Brenda with such force she had to sit down. Unfortunately, there was not a convenient chair to seat Brenda, so, unceremoniously, she found herself falling on her bottom onto the not very clean floor of the shop and if that was not embarrassing enough, she burst into uncontrollable sobs!

George looked horrified. This was completely out of his remit. What should he do with a pensioner he hardly knew who had literally collapsed at his feet in the middle of the shop and was crying so loudly he was sure the staff and customers in the Turkish Barbers next door would be able to hear? "Now, now, don't be upsetting yourself like this. It can't be that bad. Come on, let me help you up." George put his hands under her armpits and attempted to lift the collapsed form of Brenda to her feet. This proved to be a much more difficult task than he had envisaged and only resulted in him also landing on his bottom behind Brenda. The scene reminded him of the parties where he had been forced into doing the 'row boat dance' on the floor, legs either side of the person in front of him, a situation he had endured, but never enjoyed. Brenda by now had somewhat recovered herself and was struggling to regain a perpendicular position at the same time as George, ending up with knees and elbows clashing and dignities crashing.

"I am so sorry, George," Brenda said between gulps of air and sniffles, "it's just that I had my keys to my flat and my car keys in my bag, not to mention my diary and my lovely make-up bag I got from my trip to Margate and…"

George interrupted her, he was starting to panic himself, totally out of depth with this kind of situation. He still lived at home with his mother and he certainly didn't own a car. He saw them as polluting the atmosphere, choosing to walk or go on public transport instead, if forced to do so, because of constrictions of time or distance. "Right," he tried to sound authoritative and in charge of the situation, "we must ring the police and report the theft, then tackle the problem of getting into your flat. Do you leave a spare set of keys with a neighbour, friend or family?"

"Oh, I wouldn't trust my neighbours and I have never thought of leaving keys with friends. It has never crossed my mind," Brenda couldn't actually think of anyone she would call a friend, "these things don't matter, until some disaster happens. I worked with a girl who left a set of keys under a pot plant by her front door. Very foolhardy, anyone could come across them and she had told the whole office. Who is to say they were all honest?"

George, by now, was rummaging about in the backpack he had deposited on the floor, finally locating a very outmoded mobile phone with a disturbingly cracked screen. Brenda was incredulous that he was able to read any information on it. He then tapped in some numbers and waited for a response.

Suddenly, Brenda did not want the police involved. She envisaged the questioning, the look of ridicule when she would tell them where she had put her bag and the comments that would be made about looking after your valuables. She wouldn't even be able to describe a school uniform as the girls had all been swaddled in thick coasts.

"Stop, George!" she shouted, "I would rather not have the police here. It's hopeless anyway, there is nothing they can do."

George looked rather taken aback, if not a tad disappointed. He was just getting into the role of troubleshooter to be cut off in his prime. "Right, okay, erm…" George was lost for words, "I er…"

Brenda knew that George had no idea what to do, so having recovered slightly from the initial shock she attempted to think logically about the situation. She hadn't got much money in her handbag but she had a bank credit and debit card, an oyster card and various other department store cards that had been forced on her with the promise of a 10% discount on the goods she was buying. She was, in fact, quite glad they had gone. She eyed George's damaged phone. She must phone the companies immediately in case the 'Horrible Teenagers' decided to use the Oyster Card or purloin money from her account by using the contactless method available on her cards in shops. She could picture them, giggling conspiratorially as they left their chosen shops, clutching their ill-gotten gains. She had always felt uneasy with a method of payment that did not require you to put in any personal information, only a swipe of a card to activate the dots on the machine. She would refuse the facility when ordering a new card. "George, could I be so bold as to ask if I could use your phone to ring my bank and cancel my cards?"

George looked relieved that he could be of some use, handing over the cracked screen life-saver to Brenda. "Use Google to find the number you need to use to cancel them. I don't know what we'd do without Google," he added, trying to lighten the situation.

The procedure of cancelling the cards and ordering new ones was remarkably simple, leaving Brenda quite impressed. She was always wary around technology, but with George's younger brain, they managed it together. Now, back to the immediate problem of getting into Brenda's flat.

"I could always try and bash the door down." He paused as he caught Brenda eyeing his rather puny frame, even when bulked out by a duffle coat. "Or," he scratched his head, his eyes lighting up at his sudden inspiration, "we could call a locksmith." George felt quite pleased at this solution to the problem. What could be simpler?

"How do we find a locksmith at this time?" Brenda lamented, checking her watch and finding it had already turned 5:30 p.m. Where had time gone? "I expect they will have all clocked off!"

"Oh, I am sure there will be an emergency number to call," George was already tapping away at the cracked screen of his phone with dedicated fervour, "here we are, 'twenty-four-hour lock solutions, call us in all emergencies'. That should do the trick." He then continued his tapping away at the screen, ending with a long wait as the phone rang. Brenda was about to instruct him to give up on the task when she heard a muffled voice replying. George explained the situation; Brenda heard another muffled reply resulting in an exclamation of surprise or perhaps even horror emanating from George. He took the phone away from his ear. "They want a two-hundred-pound call-out fee!" He savagely scratched his head, "and he keeps calling me 'mate'," he added.

"Two hundred pounds! That is ridiculous, I would rather sleep on the streets," Brenda exclaimed, not relishing the thought of a night under the stars, "there must be another solution."

George went very quiet. This was all turning into a bit of a nightmare. He couldn't invite her back to his mother's house. She was very funny about strangers. She was ill for weeks after he had persuaded her to house an old school friend of his who had come to their area for a conference and had left it too late to book a hotel. Or, as Gorge suspected later, was pocketing the expenses and enjoying free bed and board. "Shall we walk back to your flat and see if there is an open window we could get in by?" he suggested.

"I am very careful about shutting windows. One of the neighbours lost all her jewellery and her cockatiel one summer because she left a window open to keep the room cool. We have a Neighbourhood Watch scheme now run by Richard at number fourteen. We all have a sticker on our door. We have monthly meetings. Most residents go mainly for the chocolate digestives."

George interrupted, feeling the conversation was straying from the matter in hand. "Erm, let's weigh up the situation. You have no spare keys, all your windows are shut and the locksmith costs too much. Do you know anyone who could put you up for the night and then it all can be sorted tomorrow?"

Brenda gave this question considerable thought. She had never been one for close friends. She had acquaintances but no one she felt she could call up in an emergency such as this. She felt a tinge of sadness and regret. She had spent quite a solitary life, mainly her own choice, but sometimes, just because she found it difficult to 'make friends' and keep them.

"Not really, I have always been a bit of a loner," Brenda then was suddenly struck by another problem, "My car! What if the 'Horrible Teenagers' find where my flat is and work out which is my car in the communal carpark? The key ring gives away the make of the car so they could put two and two together."

George considered this. He felt there were too many problems for him to deal with. He scratched his head, looking perplexed. "Have you got a spare pair of car keys in the flat?"

"Yes, somewhere," Brenda replied. She then was struck by an idea that came from nowhere. "The freeholder of the property, he will have a key to my flat. If we go back there, I can ask a neighbour for the number and hopefully all will be resolved."

George looked considerably relieved. "Is your flat in walking distance?"

"Yes, it should take us about twenty minutes if we get a move on." Brenda realised immediately that this was an unnecessary request as George always moved as if his life depended on it. As she imagined, George flew into action, ensuring everything was turned off or on accordingly. They were out of the door and up the High Street in minutes. He then marched her along akin to the military and they arrived at the apartment building in fifteen minutes flat, George in the lead with an exhausted Brenda trailing slightly behind. She took him up the appropriate staircase and knocked at Number 14's door. The knock was answered by a white-haired, spritely gentleman of indeterminate age, who peered around the safety chain on his door before releasing it once he had identified Brenda as being friend not foe.

"Brenda, what can I do for you? The wife and I were just having our dinner, could you come back…" Brenda cut him off.

"Sorry, Richard, I would not usually interrupt you at this time in the evening but my handbag has been stolen with my door keys and car keys and address book and I need Mr Patel's telephone number so I can ask him to come and let me into my flat. I have spare keys in there." This all came out in a torrent of words, leaving Richard a bit taken aback.

George took over. "I am George, I am the manager of the Charity Shop that Brenda volunteers in and she was very unlucky on her first day to lose her possessions. We wondered if you could help with providing us the name of your freeholder to enable her to access her flat? We would be very grateful."

Richard stepped aside, indicating for them to step over the threshold and enter the flat. George forged forward, followed by a less enthusiastic Brenda. She had never been in Richard's flat before. The Neighbourhood Watch meeting never seemed to be scheduled at Number fourteen.

When they entered the living room, they were confronted with a scenario that Brenda had never imagined or knew about. Pushed close to the dining table was a wheelchair and in the chair was a tiny lady with wispy white hair and pink-rimmed NHS glasses that gave her the look of a startled owl. She was wrapped in a soft-looking, pale blue shawl that enveloped most of her upper body and the rest was completely hidden by a long winceyette nightie. Brenda approved of this. She had one handy for cold, winter nights.

"This is Maureen. Maureen, this is Brenda from number twenty-one, upstairs with a view of the carpark and..."

"George," George helpfully intervened.

"Would you like a cup of tea?" Richard asked.

"You are in the middle of your dinner, all we wanted was the number to contact Mr Patel." She was starting to feel quite tearful now. It was probably delayed shock coupled with the realisation that she had lived for nine years in her flat without knowing that Richard had a disabled wife. Why hadn't she seen her before? Did she ever go out? Why hadn't he mentioned her?

"I will put the kettle on. You both look as if you could do with a brew." Brenda smiled ruefully. The cup of tea she had been waiting for all day, she had forgotten she even wanted one. "Take the weight off your feet, I'll be back in two minutes." Brenda never doubted that for a second. Richard had an ex-RAF look and manner about him, always standing with his shoulders back and slightly barking out his sentences as if addressing a squadron. She never felt able to oppose any of his ideas at the Neighbourhood Watch meetings. In fact, most of the attending residents were quite happy to let Richard take the helm. She didn't know what the equivalent to this would be in a plane. Something to do with the cockpit? Brenda eyed the remains of Maureen's dinner. She looked at her plate with the feeding spoon laid to one side. They had interrupted Richard feeding her. This made her feel worse. Before she could speak to Maureen, Richard was back. He put a tea tray on the table and proceeded to pour out four cups of tea. The fourth being in a feeding mug, similar to ones Brenda had witnessed young mothers using with their infant children. "Milk and sugar?" he asked.

"Just milk for me, I'm sweet enough," George attempted humour, which was ignored.

"Same here. I gave it up years ago when I was told by my dentist how bad it was for my teeth," Brenda replied, "unfortunately, I still cannot resist a nice biscuit." Richard had kindly placed a plate of the tempting articles on the tray. George had already hoovered up two of them before Brenda could make a selection. She was feeling a bit calmer now. Richard took the feeding mug over to Maureen and helped her drink it and continued to feed his wife, patiently waiting for her to chew each mouthful. Brenda drank her tea not wanting to interrupt the procedure but wondering when she could reintroduce the subject of the telephone number. It was Maureen who did that for her.

"Didn't Brenda want the telephone number of Mr Patel, Richard? Never mind me, go and see if you can find it."

Frail though she was, Maureen was obviously capable of telling Richard what to do.

Richard put down the fork and proceeded to delve into a drawer in the sideboard. He pulled out a blue file entitled 'Flat' and rummaged through its contents. "Here we are!" he triumphantly exclaimed, brandishing a piece of paper, Mr Patel 07893445609. "He only uses a mobile number. He has an e-mail address as well if…"

"No, that's fine. I never was one for computers. Is it okay if I phone him now, Richard? George, can I use your mobile phone again?"

"Be my guest," George handed over the cracked screen to Brenda who was making a mental note to buy him a new screen for all the help he was giving her today.

"Thank you, George. Well, here goes," Brenda painstakingly tapped the numbers in, screwing up her eyes to enable her to see the screen. Her magnifiers were, of course, in her handbag. The phone dutifully rang and was at last answered by a rather bad-tempered voice that seemed to be coming from inside a cupboard. Brenda went into a detailed description of the missing handbag and the need to access the flat with his keys but was interrupted by Mr Patel.

"I am in Birmingham and will not be back until tomorrow afternoon. I will wait for you at five o'clock tomorrow outside your flat. In future, please leave a key with a neighbour. This is all most inconvenient."

Brenda felt like a small child being told off. "Thank you, Mr Patel. That is very kind of you. I will see you tomorrow." It wasn't until she had handed the phone back to George that she realised she still had nowhere to sleep that night.

Chapter 3

Brenda and George said their goodbyes to Richard and Maureen. Brenda most certainly did not want to burden them any further with the pending question of Brenda's accommodation. She wondered if George was aware of the problem. By the time they had reached the communal entrance of the flats, Brenda had images of railway arches, shop doors and hostels. It was a cold evening that was likely to turn into a very cold night. Brenda shivered at the thought. Then she had an idea. Rather than a shop door, what if she slept in the Charity Shop itself? The back room was stacked with linens. There was probably a duvet in there and pillows, yes, she could make herself quite *comfortable* and it would only be for one night until Mr Patel returned from Birmingham. She felt quite elated. It would be quite an adventure.

"George, I've had an idea that could solve my present predicament. I've nowhere to go tonight and wondered if I could sleep in the backroom of the shop. There must be bedding and I could lay out the cushions I saw in a pile in the corner waiting to be priced, to act as a mattress. I could nip to Sainsbury's and buy myself some food and there is of course a kettle and tea bags and I assume there must be milk?" This all came out in such a rush she felt quite breathless. George, however, looked winded. He stopped in his tracks, frantically scratched his head and then started to pace backwards and forwards, muttering something about health and safety and risking his job and 'Mother' came into it somewhere. He finally wound down and came to a halt.

"I er...I don't know, Brenda, it all sounds highly irregular. Is there no other solution?"

"Not unless you can think of one. It would be quite an adventure, a bit like the Brownie camping holidays I went on as a child. Well, that was under canvas in a field with cows treacherously close, but I loved the sense of danger. Nobody would know I was there and I would be all tidied away by the morning shift," Brenda looked expectantly at George who was now studying his watch.

"Mother will be worrying where I am. I suppose there is no other way around this. I will give her a quick ring then open up the shop for you. I can lend you some money from today's takings to get in provisions, no fish and chips, though, we don't want the shop smelling of grease and vinegar. Alan will know there has been someone in there. He may have problems with his hearing, but I do not think that extends to his sense of smell." George, by now, had resumed his cracking pace and they soon reached the shop. He searched for and found the shop keys that seemed to be attached to a long piece of string that ended its journey in one of the pockets of George's Paddington Bear coat. It reminded Brenda of the pieces of elastic her mother used to thread through the arms of her school coat with her gloves tied to the end of them to stop her losing them when she wasn't wearing them. He eventually got access to the shop and ran in to turn off the alarm. She entered behind him, wondering whether this was a good idea after all. *Oh well,* she thought for the second time that day, *Needs must.*

It seemed very gloomy and a bit sinister in the shop. The light was failing and shadows were being cast against the walls. The ever-present smell of the second-hand clothes seemed worse than through the day and she thought back to one of the 'Horrible Teenagers' remarking about the sweaty trainers. She pushed the thought of the girls from her mind. She must start to be practical. She was glad when George went home to mother, his head scratching and constant nervous energy could be tiring. She would slip to Sainsburys, buy herself something tasty for her dinner then sort herself out for the evening's vigil.

George had no intention of tarrying any longer than he needed to, so after issuing Brenda with a verbal list of what not to do or turn on or off and passing her some money from a cash box, he disappeared up the road at lightning speed. Brenda was on her own.

Brenda was very used to her own company. She was an only child. "We tried for another baby," her mother had explained to her when she asked why everyone in her class had brothers and sisters except for her, "but it never happened, so we had to be content with just you." Brenda thought she detected a note of disappointment in her mother's voice, as if the situation was an unsatisfactory compromise. Then, as she got older and watched the other girls getting 'silly' about boys, Brenda remained aloof and out of the situation. The boys never looked at her and she, in turn, wasn't really interested in them. They all seemed so immature with their loud voices and spotty faces. Hence, she never got married and when she eventually left home, encouraged constantly by her mother, she had lived in flats closest to her work, staying in the last one after her retirement. No, she was better on her own.

She had never done a night shop at Sainsburys. She hadn't needed to. The clientele was different. These were mainly young, city workers who had finished a day's work, suffered the gruelling tube and train journey home only to realise they needed to shop if they were to eat that night or drink a glass or two of wine to obliterate the strains and stresses of the day. The queues were short and Brenda was around in no time and was soon walking back to the shop with a prawn layer salad, a strawberry yoghurt and a 'reduced item' mille-feuille that looked a bit worse for wear as the cream had started to ooze out of the sides. *But it all goes down the same way*, thought Brenda.

She let herself back into the shop, turning off the alarm as George had instructed and went into the back room, shutting the door before turning on the light, in case some keen policeman should think there was an intruder. She put down her shopping, took off her coat, and set about finding cutlery, a mug, milk and tea bags. All except the tea bags were easy to locate and she finally tracked down the latter in a white tin with red letters stating 'Saved for a Rainy Day'. The milk was just on the cusp of turning sour but *Beggars can't be choosers*, reasoned Brenda.

She found a *comfortable* chair to consume her picnic meal, managing to get the cream from the mille-feuille down her cardigan. She hadn't realised how hungry she was. She hadn't had anything since the cereal bar she had hastily eaten before leaving home for the Charity Shop. She put all the packaging in the carrier bag she had reluctantly purchased at the supermarket. She always carried a bag for life, but that was in the missing handbag. What else would she discover she had lost? "I'll make a list of all the contents of my bag to enable me to replace everything," Brenda said out loud, then quickly reminded herself that she must not make any noise. She giggled (silently), she felt like a naughty schoolgirl.

The time had come when she must find the necessary bed linen for her night's stay. The duvet and cover were easily accessible but the pillows were harder to locate. In the end, she settled on a large soft cushion and used the rest of the cushions to form a mattress, as she had planned. She tested it out for comfort. She liked a hard mattress, so the floor under the cushions had this effect. *That'll do,* she thought, glancing at her watch and finding it was only 8:05 p.m. *Too early for bed yet.*

She caught sight of a teetering pile of books in a corner. She ran her eyes down the selection of authors and finally settled for a Mann Brooker Prize winner she had not read or even heard of. She settled back down in the comfortable chair and proceeded to read. She just about managed without her magnifiers. That reminded her, she must make that list. The book was intriguing and time flew. The next thing Brenda was aware of was a low rhythmic beat that sounded as if it was coming from the shop. Brenda froze. Had someone got in? Had she inadvertently left the door open? She rose from her chair quietly, laying the book to one side and crept towards the door. As noiselessly as she could, she opened the door and attempted to peer through it. Nothing. Only darkness and the lights from the road lamps and car headlights giving some relief.

Then she opened the door enough to enable her to squeeze out and enter the shop floor, quickly closing it behind her to obliterate the electric light. She hesitantly walked across the shop floor following the music, then stopped before she reached the window. Then, outside the shop door, she saw it. A bundle of bedding, carrier bags and a figure intent on trying to light a roll up with his hands cupped against the breeze. He managed at last and inhaled a lung-full of smoke, letting it out bit by bit with obvious satisfaction. He then crawled inside his duvet, Brenda was amused to see it was a leopard skin design clashing with a pink Barbie pillowcase, pulling a red, woolly, bobble hat over his head, covering his ears. He reached for the source of the music Brenda had heard, a rather grubby-looking CD player and pulled it closer to his ears. Brenda was struck with the similarity of his and her situation. Both with nowhere to sleep through the night, ending up at the Charity Shop. One inside, one outside. For a moment, Brenda froze on the spot. Should she open the door and let him into the relatively warm shop to sleep the night? She quickly came to her senses. A stranger she had never set eyes on before, that would be asking for trouble, she told herself as she retreated into her backroom sanctuary.

Her tea had gone cold and there was not much milk left. She assumed George or one of the morning shifts would be ascribed to bring in a new carton of milk in the morning. She attempted to settle down to reading again but found her concentration had been shattered by the low beat of the music outside and the shock of her surprise 'companion'. She felt guilty that she was in the comparative warmth and he was outside bundled up in leopard skin print, in the cold of the evening, which would only get worse as night set in.

Pushing these thoughts to one side, Brenda decided to write a list of the contents of her handbag, she mustn't put it off any longer. At least she had cancelled her bank card, otherwise the 'Horrible Teenagers' could have cleared her bank account by now, just with one large shop at Primark. She found a pen and some paper fairly easily and settled back down in her *comfortable* chair. She entitled it 'Lost', underlining it for emphasis.

LOST

Leather purse – contents: £25.60, NatWest debit card, Costa Rewards Card, library card, Oyster card, various chain store cards, too many to remember and never used.

Makeup purse – contents: lipstick, handbag mirror, Miniature folding umbrella.

Bag for life. A pen and pencil.

Address book. Key ring with her flat keys and car keys.

Magnifiers.

A tube of extra strong mints (opened and mainly consumed). A plastic spoon (for use in Costas as they only provided wooden sticks, which she found intolerable.) A cereal bar for emergencies.

Brenda considered the list. There was probably more but she couldn't bring them to mind at the moment. It didn't seem too bad she concluded. She might even enjoy buying the replacements. Having done this, she washed her mug up in the inadequately sized sink and visited the tiny toilet with its grubby looking hand towel, making a mental note to take it back with her once she had access to her flat, and launder it. She then attempted to prepare herself for the night ahead. She had locked the front door and she knew George had checked the back one. She opened the door of her improvised bedroom a fraction to reveal the shape of her visitor outside the shop. The music had stopped and all was quiet out there. There was no movement so she assumed he had fallen asleep. Oh well, she might as well attempt the same. Thinking this, she removed her cardigan, shoes and tights, turned off the light and slid under the duvet.

Chapter 4

She must have been very tired because the next thing she was aware of was the sound of voices and a key in the lock. Brenda couldn't work out why anyone would be entering her flat and she swung her legs around to get out of bed to find she was on the floor. She realised where she was and the ridiculousness of the situation. She hauled herself up to a standing position, feeling slightly dizzy and disorientated, running her fingers through her hair that seemed to be standing on end. With no mirror to hand she could only guess how awful she must look. *There must surely be a mirror for sale in the shop somewhere?* Putting aside the uncomfortable thought of not being able to have a shower until after 5 p.m. that evening, she folded up her improvised bedding. *I will take it home and wash it tonight,* she thought, and prepared to face George.

She opened the backroom door. There, fiddling with the key that appeared to refuse to be extracted from the door, was a figure that certainly was not the wiry frame of George. This was unmistakeably female, squat and matronly, she was wrapped up in a beige trench coat with the belt knotted at the front and a woolly Fair Isle patterned, probably hand knitted hat pulled down over her ears. Brenda made a mental note to ask her for the knitting pattern then corrected herself as she guessed she probably bought it from the Charity Shop. She was making noises of frustration as the key was proving a problem and Brenda felt she ought to make herself known as she stood awkwardly in the background.

"Erm, hello," ventured Brenda as she approached the battling figure who, with one last effort, managed to get the key out of the lock and almost in one action ran to turn off the alarm, the effort of which seemed to quite floor her as she leant against the nearest wall to catch her breath. Then she caught sight of the speechless Brenda.

"What the…!" she gasped, "who the 'ell are you, how did you get in? You gave me the fright of my life, you could have been the end of me," she accusingly blurted out, still retaining her position with her back to the wall, staring at Brenda as if she had arrived from another planet.

"I am so sorry," Brenda began, "I was expecting George. He knows I'm here. I regretfully had my handbag stolen yesterday with all my keys, money and cards and was left in the dubious position of having no means of entering my establishment or my car so I slept here last night on my own, well, except for," she glanced out of the window, no sign of her fellow homeless companion, "a gentleman who was sleeping in the doorway."

"Oh, that would be Patrick, he likes our doorway, says it is sheltered from the wind and rain, nice bloke, a bit too familiar with the drink, but when he is sober, he can tell you many a tale of his time in the army. He refuses to go into a hostel, says they smell of pee and they don't let him drink," she sighed, shaking her head and at last peeling herself from the wall and simultaneously unknotting her coat belt before removing the coat itself which she draped over the nearest clothes rack. "So what's your name then? You volunteering here or was you an unlucky punter?"

"The former," Brenda replied, allowing herself to step further into the shop, "it was my first day, such bad luck. It will all be sorted this evening when the freeholder of my flat returns from Birmingham with my key," she explained in a rush of words. "I assume you're a volunteer too? I am not supposed to be working today but I am rendered actionless until I get into my flat, I wondered er…" Brenda trailed off, realising that she had a long time to fill in until 5 o'clock, she began again, "I thought maybe I could make myself useful here? Emptying the bags or hanging garments on rails or…"

"Well, Alan will be 'ere at ten o clock. He is on the morning shift with me and then Linda should arrive at 1 p.m. for the afternoon shift, if she is well enough. George gets in a bit later on a Tuesday as he takes 'is mum to 'er Scrabble club. I am sure there will be 'somefink' you can do, never say no to an extra pair of 'ands. You could start by puttin' the kettle on."

Brenda felt herself blush. She had finished the milk last night with her copious cups of tea. She had not thought for a moment about the following day's shift. She would have to dash out to Sainsburys.

"I am so sorry," Brenda blurted out, "I finished the milk last night but I'll pop out to the supermarket and purchase some more." Brenda suddenly realised she did not know the volunteer's name or introduced herself. "I am Brenda, by the way, and you are?"

"Call me Queenie," she replied, "it's really Victoria but I prefer Queenie, my dad called me it when I was a nipper and it kind of stuck." She chortled, "He reckoned I ruled him, I was the apple of 'is eye."

"I haven't any money, Queenie, George lent me some last night but I've exhausted that, I couldn't ask you to lend me some until I'm able to obtain some funds?"

"You don't half talk posh!" Queenie exclaimed, "no problem about the milk. One person on duty brings in a fresh carton each day. It's my turn today. We get through a 'lor' of tea and coffee particularly, Alan. I reckon he only comes in for the tea and a chat. Loves a custard cream biscuit as well, I've known him down four in one tea break. Don't reckon he looks after himself very well. 'is wife died last year. They did 'everyfing' together. That's when he started 'ere." She looked quite wistful, "Miss my Brian. He's been gone six years next January. Massive 'eart attack in front of the betting shop in Culvert Street, must 'ave put the punters off. Out the blue it was, 'e was as 'ealthy as an horse, played bowls, did the garden, played for hours with the grandchildren. You never know what's 'round the corner, do you?"

Brenda shook her head, sagely, not really knowing how to reply to this revelation of Queenie's home life. Never having had a husband herself, she felt unqualified to answer. "I'll put the kettle on then if you can let me have the milk?" Brenda asked. She approached the backroom briskly. Queenie picked up her shopping bag and brought out a carton of semi-skimmed and as she was handing it to Brenda, in strode Alan, on cue, muffled up in a thick scarf, coat and flat cap.

"Must 'ave heard the kettle boiling," Queenie exclaimed. "Is that right, Alan, you 'eard the kettle was on. You ready for a cuppa?" Queenie had raised her voice to a near shout, Brenda remembered Alan was hard of hearing.

"Wouldn't say no, you know me, never turn down a brew." He looked at Brenda, "I know you, don't I? You were in yesterday to see George about volunteering. Are you with us this morning then? I thought it was just you, Linda and me, Queenie?" Alan looked quite disappointed that the threesome was being threatened by an outsider. "Too many cooks spoil the broth, my old mother used to say."

"She's had a bit of bad luck yesterday, 'ad 'er 'and bag stolen with 'er keys and money and everything in it. She stayed 'ere the night, with George's permission, of course," she added, probably before Alan asked it. "Another pair of 'ands is always welcome. Alan 'as three sugars in a milky tea, Brenda, and mine is a coffee with no sugar, just milk. You will find the biscuits in the cupboard above the fridge. There should be a plate there as well unless George 'as sold it. I have 'ad two mugs go that way."

Brenda busied herself with the drinks, she could hear Queenie and Alan talking in the shop – Alan rather loudly and knew it was about her. Memories of being talked about at work by the younger members of staff flooded back. Still, she was here for the day, if she didn't like it, she could leave and find some other voluntary work. She went through the other possibilities she had considered before choosing the Charity Shop. Driving elderly or disabled people to the shops, helping out at National Trust Houses, clearing rivers or woodland of weeds – that sounded a bit too strenuous for her; being an usher at the Globe in London – that sounded good as she could see the Shakespeare plays, but a long way to get there and back. No, this suited her. She completed the tea-making task and returned to the shop bearing the mugs and biscuits on a tray she had found on the floor with no price on it, so presumably available for use.

As soon as she entered the shop floor, Queenie and Alan ceased their chat and took their tea. "Thanks, love, this is very welcome," said Queenie, "as soon as we've finished this, we can start on them black bin liners that bloke brought in yesterday, about six of 'em there were. Posh geezer 'e was, suit and tie, hoity toity accent. Lovely car. Parked on double yellers without a worry in the world. Bet there's some good stuff in them bags." She took a sip of coffee, decided it was too hot and put it on the counter. "We send items that are really good to be put on eBay, Brenda. Get more money that way and some we send to other stores if we think the stuff will go quicker there."

Alan, meanwhile, was attacking the plate of biscuits with gusto, dunking them into his tea before consumption. "A bit strong this tea," he complained, "are you sure you put in three sugars?" he questioned, frowning at the mug as if it had plotted his downfall.

"I'm sure I did, Alan," Brenda replied apologetically, "do you want me to make you another one?"

"It'll have to do; I'll make the next round and show you how it's done. There is a knack to it."

Brenda wondered what on earth the knack was. Alan obviously treated the making of tea like a specialised talent, only accessible to those in the know. *Oh, well, let him have his moment.* "I'll look forward to that, Alan," Brenda replied, trying to sound enthusiastic rather than sarcastic.

Queenie had disappeared into the backroom and Alan looked at his watch and moved towards the shop's front doors. He opened these and came back to 'force down' the unsatisfactory tea. There were sounds of 'oohs' and 'aahs' coming from Queenie as she rustled her way through the bags she had mentioned. "You've 'gotta' see this lot!" she shouted. "Bleeding treasure trove 'ere. My Brian would've loved all this. Real gentleman's clobber, this lot, and some lovely pottery, lamps, watches, playing cards cigarette 'olders and," she paused, "some lovely framed photos, 'spect they're his family. One of them Victorian photos where they never smiled, I bet this lot is worth a pretty penny."

The shop was now open and people had started to wander in, so Brenda thought she had better not retreat into the backroom. She was about to ask Alan whether she should go behind the till, but curiosity had obviously been too much for Alan to resist and he too disappeared into the backroom. Brenda made her own decision and stood behind the till hoping she looked confident and in charge, although she felt neither. One of the customers walked in with a rather overweight chocolate Labrador. Brenda didn't know if dogs were allowed in the shop, but going off the owner's authoritarian manner, she assumed this had occurred on numerous previous occasions. The dog then proceeded to approach Brenda and he lay on its back with the obvious aim of encouraging Brenda to tickle his tummy. The gender became apparent once the dog lay with its genitalia exposed to the elements. Brenda had never had a dog. Her father used to say they were a tie and who would walk it every day and pick up its mess. Not him, that was for sure. So the family remained 'petless'. Brenda stooped to oblige the panting dog whilst its owner perused the merchandise.

"He's very friendly and loves his tummy being tickled," a female voice informed Brenda. "He would let you do that all day if you were willing," she added. Her voice was soprano, well, squeaky if she was to be honest. The voice appeared from behind a clothes rail which was not much shorter than her. She was wearing a blue mackintosh tied severely around the middle with a matching belt. Her shoes were sturdy and her tights woollen and she had a scarf of vast proportions wrapped around her neck that also covered her ears. Brenda was surprised she was able to hear a thing through it. Even though she was obviously sorting through the clothes rails, she still had a pair of sheepskin mittens on, but seemed to be managing satisfactorily. Brenda straightened up and smiled at the dog owner.

"He's called Buster. Used to be a real Buster at one time, couldn't let him off the lead in case he saw off all the local dogs and cats. He was always fine with people though, gentle as a lamb but a sniff of another animal he was off, wanting to fight with them. He's mellowed with age though. He hasn't got the energy. A bit like me really," she added, "we've grown old together, haven't we, Buster?" She rubbed Buster's back thoughtfully, "I've often wondered who will go first, him or me. I will be eighty-nine next birthday."

Realising this was a cue for a response, Brenda joined in appropriately, "Well, you certainly don't look eighty-nine. You look half that age." Perhaps this was a tad too much but the dog owner looked pleased. It was at this moment that realisation struck Brenda. She knew this lady. Something about the aquiline nose and sharp features, even her hair scraped back in a bun was familiar. Then it came to her like a bolt of lightning. She used to be her English teacher at Christchurch High School. Brenda had left there at eighteen. That was forty-two years ago, so if the dog owner was eighty-nine, she would have been forty-seven when she left. That seemed about right. What was her name? She wasn't married then and because of the sheepskin gloves, she couldn't see if this status had changed in the intermittent years. She stood gaping, mouth open, not really sure what to say or do, if anything. She was sure the name began with a 'T'. It would come back to her later. She remembered she was a strict teacher, lines and detentions were liberally distributed at the slight hint of dissent or disobedience. The memory of spending a long hour in the detention room for incomplete homework or failing a spelling test still haunted Brenda. Then she remembered something else. A hot summer day with inadequate ventilation, reading 'Hamlet' around the class, so bored, wanting to be anywhere but in the classroom. She remembered the discussion afterwards about the school play which would be, as it was every year, the set

A Level Shakespeare play, so this year it would be 'Hamlet'. She remembered putting her hand up and asking why it had to be a Shakespeare play? Couldn't they do a modern playwright?

The silence after the remark was chilling. Miss 'T' put down her copy of the play and stared with tangible hostility at Brenda. She then addressed the stunned girls, "I have been teaching here for twenty-six years and we have always done a Shakespeare school play and I am sure that will be the case for the next twenty-six years." Brenda could still hear those words to this day. After that, Miss 'T' treated her as if she came from some unworthy social class not to be spoken to and needless to say, she never got a role in a school play again, but that came as some relief to Brenda who had no desire to tread the boards. She ended up either prompting or helping with costumes, jobs no one else wanted. This suited her fine.

She was brought back to the present by the sound of the telephone in the backroom. She had forgotten that Queenie and Alan were still in there sorting out the bags. The phone was answered and the voice of Queenie could be heard obviously arguing with someone on the other end. "I cannot do a 'fing' about it, mate. Your brother dropped 'em off at the shop and we've already asked for some items to be put on eBay. Some nice clobber." Whoever was on the other end of telephone had interrupted and Queenie was cut off by whatever they were saying. "You'll have to sort that out 'wiv' him mate. Not my problem." She then put the phone back. "Would you Adam and Eve it. One 'brover' brings in a load of stuff belonging to his old dad and the other 'brover' wants it all back! Says it should go the grandchildren. Well, nothing to do with me, they can sort themselves out."

Alan then appeared looking slightly dazed. He was holding a rather smart briefcase in brown leather. It hardly looked used. "Shame about that, Queenie, I was going to buy this one myself. Always wanted a leather briefcase but we got synthetic ones at work. They always were cheapskates. Oh well, I'd better start putting everything back into the bags. Just came out to see what you were up to," he addressed Brenda, "can you manage for ten more minutes? It was a good thing after all that we are overstaffed," he admitted begrudgingly. With that, he and the briefcase disappeared again, leaving Brenda with Miss 'T' who had been listening to the exchange whilst continuing her search through the rails.

"This looks warm," she said, holding up a pale pink cardigan, buttoned up to the neck and obviously hand-knitted, probably for a loved one who never wore it, secreting it to a charity shop at the first possible opportunity. "I'll just slip it on for the fit." At which point she took off her scarf, coat, gloves and a very similar cardigan, all of which she hung over nearby rails and slipped on the new cardigan, making sure the buttons were aligned with the button holes. She then found the one mirror in the shop and appraised the result, turning left and right to see the effect from different angles. "I'm not sure it is my colour; I tend to stick to blues but it is warm." Brenda wasn't sure if she was talking to herself or to her but thought she should try and offer some encouragement for Miss 'T' to buy the garment so that at least she had made a sale.

"I think it really suits you," she offered, "It hardly looks worn."

"Hmmmm," came the response, "I'll think about it." She began unbuttoning the cardigan. Then donned her own clothes in the reverse order in which she removed them. "Come on, Buster," she checked her watch, "time to go to the dentist. They will be open now." She then gathered Buster up from his recumbent position and left the shop.

Brenda could not help but think she was only filling in time before her dental appointment, somewhere warmer than the chilly Tuesday morning on the High Street. It wasn't until the tiny figure and trundling Labrador had disappeared from view that Brenda remembered the name of her former teacher. Miss Tottle, that was it. Brenda giggled to herself. The girls in her class used to call her 'Miss Tottle in full Throttle' when she got angry with them. Perhaps she would acknowledge she knew her next time she was in the shop. Or perhaps not. *The past is in the past,* she thought.

There were not many people in the shop and they looked as if they were only sheltering from the cold, on their way somewhere else, like Miss Tottle. She could hear Queenie and Alan filling up bags in the backroom. She was suddenly aware she was hungry. It was a long time since her prawn layer supper and she had missed her porridge and blueberries at breakfast time. She should have got to the custard creams before Alan had consumed them all. She couldn't ask either of them, it was too embarrassing. George would be in soon and as he had already lent her some money he might do so again unasked and she could at least buy some lunch.

She was contemplating what she would eat later on when the sounds of angry voices in the doorway of the shop brought her back down to earth. There were two middle-aged men outside, both wearing what looked like Burberry coats and scarves, smart trousers and stylish shoes. Brenda had seen this kind of men's wear in shops in the West End, rarely locally. Both of them were red in the face, either from the cold or overindulgence of port, but more likely from anger and frustration. She couldn't hear what they were saying very clearly, even though they were shouting, as the windows were double-glazed, but she assumed these were the warring brothers, horns locked over the question of their father's possessions. She left the till to open the backroom door wide enough to announce to Queenie and Alan that the brothers had arrived, returning immediately to her post. There were the sounds of bags being pulled along the floor and a continuous exchange between the two annoyed volunteers. They did not appreciate the extra work thrust on them. To unpack and sort so many bags, put some of them on eBay and then have to repack them all again and take them off eBay, was no small task and neither of them were spring chickens. With Brenda's help, they managed to deposit the haul in the middle of the shop, issuing warnings to other customers that the goods were not for sale.

Literally, at the same moment, the brothers entered the shop, both pushing each other to be the first to put forward their claim to the booty. Other customers moved to one side, taking a front-row view of the ensuing drama. They were not disappointed. Brother One grabbed as many bags as he could manage whilst Brother Two attempted to remove these from his grasp at the same time as he rescued the remaining ones. This resulted in bags being torn open, their contents spilling unceremoniously onto the shop floor. It was at this moment that the Burberry Brothers looked at each other and then at the gaping eyes around them, realising how undignified they were appearing to the hoi polloi. Brother One coughed and loosened his tie. Brenda was glad about this, as he had looked near to a heart attack.

"Now, George, this is ridiculous. I don't know what you will do with all this tut. Don't you think Father would have preferred us to donate it all to a worthy cause, rather than have it rotting away in a garage or loft somewhere in the faint and unrealistic hope that one of the grandchildren would want it? Why not leave it all here and be content it is something Father would have done himself?"

"That is absolute rot and you know it, Simon. There was not a charitable bone in Father's body. He will be spinning in his grave at the thought of what you are doing. No, I think we ought to take it back and sort it out properly and if there is anything we know the family will definitely not want then we can return. You didn't even tell me what you were doing with the stuff. What right had you to do that? Oh, and don't throw the old adage of 'I'm the eldest' at me. I've had that since I was born."

"You had nothing to do with Father after Mum died, you always were a mummy's boy, it was me and Eileen who did everything for him." Brenda assumed this was his wife. "So, don't start criticising what decisions I made at the time, you were nowhere to be seen!"

The Burberry Brothers, hands on hips, stared at each other threateningly. There was a pause, before Queenie, who was getting tired of the ridiculous argument, broke in,

"When you two 'ave finished fighting, we 'ave a shop to run so take your bags and scarper. In future, sort yourselves out before plonking your stuff on us. We aint 'ere for our 'ealth, you know. You toffs are all the same, expecting everyone else to do the work for you and…" She was interrupted mid-sentence by Simon who was scanning the piles of bags and the rest of the shop.

"The lampstand with the onyx base and silk shade. It isn't here. Do any of you know where it was put?"

Queenie and Alan looked at each other. Both shook their heads. "There was nothing like that as far as I know," Alan retorted. *Rather defensively,* Brenda thought. "I'd have remembered one of them. We don't often get them in nowadays."

Queenie said nothing, remaining, with arms folded in front of the backroom door, as if daring the brothers to search in there for the missing article.

"It was very valuable," continued Simon who was sensing animosity amongst the volunteers. "If you come across it, can you give me a ring?" he handed Alan what looked like his business card. Alan pocketed it and remained silent. The rest of the customers, sensing the drama was over, continued to browse, or left to continue their shopping elsewhere. The brothers set about gathering the bags continuing to bicker quietly to each other. They had obviously ignored the double yellow lines and had parked right outside the shop in their considerably expensive looking cars. When the job was completed, Brenda had no idea how they divided their father's goods, probably by splitting the number of bags in half…hopefully there was an even number.

As the last bag disappeared, George appeared, looking his usual flustered self, wrapped in his Paddington duffle coat and clutching a Tesco bag that had seen better days. He held the door open for the last brother to exit as he entered, staring after them quizzically. "Shouldn't they be bringing bags in not taking them out?" he asked, looking quite bemused.

"You don't 'wanner' know," Queenie offered in reply, "it's all sorted now, just a mix up 'tween two idiots who need their 'eads banging together. 'ow's yer mother, George?"

"She was not feeling too good today," George replied fretfully, "hence why I am so late. Her dental plate needs fixing, got a crack in it or something, so I had to sort out a dentist's appointment before taking her to her Scrabble Club. Then when we got there, her friend Rita hadn't turned up and she said no one else ever spoke to her and she didn't want to stay, so I had to take her home again, make her a cup of tea and get the right channel for 'The Price is Right' before I could leave her!"

Brenda felt for him, she remembered experiencing these sorts of problems when her mother was left alone after the death of her father. As an only child, she was always obliged to attend every demand made of her. Phone calls in the middle of the night, or worse, when she was at work, often in the middle of a meeting. She learnt to turn off her phone and pick the plaintive messages up later.

Queenie took over. "You 'ave a sit down in the back and I'll make you a nice brew," she said steering George as a mother would a child to the backroom, "I'll be back in a tick. Let me know if there is 'ow't you can't 'andle." This was directed, Brenda assumed, at her.

As the door closed to the back room, Brenda could just make out George exclaiming to Queenie, "That's a beautiful lamp stand, who brought that in?"

Chapter 5

Alan assumed the role of till attendant presumably through authority gained from length of employment, so Brenda, surplus to requirements, wandered around the shop, straightening the rails, aligning the bric-a-brac and putting books into alphabetical order of the author. Alan was peering out of the window at the dismal grey skies and that imminently threatened a downpour of rain. Brenda was reminded of her telescopic umbrella, probably being brandished by the 'Horrible Teenagers' at this very moment. *Oh well,* she thought, *let's hope it's blown over by lunchtime.*

"Mmm," Alan broke the silence, "we'll be getting in all the straddlers looking for somewhere to shelter from the rain. Never buy a thing, just stay long enough to let the rain clouds pass over, then scarper. I'd charge 'em a couple of quid for the privilege. That would stop 'em." Brenda was about to comment that they would probably never come in again to purchase an item and might tell all their friends to select another charity shop to spend their money in, but she didn't. Instead, she changed the subject.

"How long have you been volunteering here, Alan?"

"Too long," he replied, abruptly, "I'm getting too old for all this standing up behind a till. Worse still, they asked me to do a session of shaking the tin the other weekend. I ask you, at my age? Nearly killed me. Couldn't find a sheltered spot to stand other than shop doorways. I stood in Santander's entrance for a while but a young Whipper Snapper came out to say I was blocking the entrance and could I move away? I felt like a tramp being moved on by a copper." He paused for a while and for a moment, Brenda thought he had nodded off. "Mind you, I have met some surprising people. Once, this really tall blonde came up, talking about how she was very interested in raising money for cancer as her sister had breast cancer but was in remission after treatment. Talking for ages she was, then this bloke comes up, I recognised him immediately, really famous in the seventies, still does tours you know the one I mean." Alan then began to sing a song Brenda was familiar with, in a slightly off-tune voice. She smiled benevolently, waiting for him to end this rather painful rendition. "He was in a rush to get somewhere though, so he dipped in his pocket and put a fifty pence coin in the tin. I ask you," Alan exclaimed, "a bleeding fifty pence with all his millions, it's always the rich that are the meanest." He took out the familiar, grubby handkerchief and gave his nose a resounding blow and tucked it away for later use.

Relieved that the singing, if you could call it that, had stopped, particularly as two potential customers had fled the shop, Brenda changed the subject. "Have you ever had any surprising donations since you have been here?" she asked.

Alan considered this question for quite a time, to the point where Brenda thought he either hadn't heard her. Then he chuckled to himself. "Couple of years ago," he shuffled himself into a conspiratorial position, leaning over the counter and lowering his voice to almost a whisper to the point where Brenda had to move closer to the till to enable her to hear. "I was out the back sorting the latest contributions. There was a lady manageress then, Marjorie, I think her name was, nice little lady, only about five foot two tall, I started on a big box that looked as if it had never been opened. Had to get the scissors to cut the sealing tape and you can never find a pair when you want them." He then went into a paroxysmal attack of coughing ending up with the necessity of using the grubby handkerchief once again. Brenda wished he would get on with his story. She was starting to feel a bit faint from lack of food and sleep. "I opened it at last," Alan continued, "and inside the box were lots of different shaped parcels wrapped in brown paper. I remember thinking that it was a long time since I had seen any brown wrapping paper. Everything now is in plastic bags helping to pollute the environment," he added vehemently. "Anyway, using the scissors again I managed to open up one parcel and you will never guess in a month of Sundays what was inside!" he paused for dramatic effect. Brenda wasn't sure if she was supposed to voice a guess but remained silent. She had no idea what the parcels contained and at this moment in time, she really didn't have the energy to care. "Toys for adults. You know what I mean? Naughty toys for adults," Alan winked conspiratorially, "to be used in the bedroom," he added finally.

Brenda had no idea what he was talking about. She knew some people had televisions in their bedrooms or books to read, discarded after a few chapters as they nodded off, but toys? She tried to imagine any toy that an adult might enjoy at night and could only think of board games like Scrabble or perhaps Solitaire. Alan, noting Brenda's blank expression, filled in the missing information, leaning near to her ear so the remaining two customers couldn't hear him, "Sex aids," he hissed, "you know what I mean? I hadn't seen anything like them since my days in the navy." He laughed to himself at this, so much that it brought on another bout of coughing and another appearance of the grubby handkerchief. Brenda meanwhile was quite shocked. Who would donate such things to a charity shop? She felt quite uncomfortable discussing such things but Alan ploughed on undeterred. "I left a vibrator with a willy warmer on it in Marjorie's office, just for a joke but she never even mentioned it. Probably didn't know what it was for," another burst of laughter from Alan, "I couldn't take 'em home for the misses. She'd have kicked me out of the house! Binned 'em all in the end. I often imagined some poor sod wondering what had happened to his hoard. Probably his mother or wife had got rid of them before they could be used." Having finished his tale and disappointed at Brenda's blank reaction he moved away. "Fancy a cuppa?" he threw back over his shoulder. "Must be about that time," he added, "I finish at one and then Linda will be in. If she is well enough. She's between treatments at the moment, poor girl. I'll wait until she arrives and I can always stay the afternoon if she doesn't." With that, he disappeared and seconds later, George, as flustered as ever, appeared having finished his tête-à-tête with Queenie.

"Sorry, Brenda, I feel as if I have neglected you, especially after your traumatic experience yesterday. Mother is being so difficult at the moment and…" He trailed off looking tormented and scratching his head with vigour, "Anyway, how was your night in the backroom? I hope you got some sleep? I did think of you when I got up at about two in the morning to refill Mother's hot water bottle that had gone cold on her."

"I was fine, George. There was a young man in the doorway with a portable radio but he had gone by the morning. Thank you for all your help yesterday and for lending me some money to buy my supper." Brenda hoped this might spur in George the realisation that she might be needing more sustenance. This was not the case, as George's eyes were elsewhere. A tall woman had entered the shop. She had gold shoes on, skinny pale blue jeans, that fitted her perfectly, and a brown leather belt that matched her clutch purse and waist-level jacket. This was topped by a long, silk scarf wrapped casually but stylishly around her neck. Her hair was coiffured into a French plait at the back of her head and held in place by a silver hair clasp that had the shapes of three shields on it. *She is*, Brenda ruefully thought, *Miss Perfect*.

George was positively mesmerised. He scratched his head a few times and then darted out to take command of the till to enable him to have a full view of 'Miss Perfect' and be able to take and wrap her purchases. Brenda did not know whether to laugh at this puppy-like devotion or cry at the ridiculous idea that she would be for one moment interested in George. She thought about taking him to one side and suggesting he was 'punching above his weight'. Then again, it was nothing to do with her but she felt a motherly concern for George and didn't want him to make a fool of himself so she joined him at the till. He didn't acknowledge her presence but remained transfixed, watching 'Miss Perfect's' every move. She wandered around, pausing for a while at the locked glass cabinet that held the more valuable articles. "Is this a Lladro?" she enquired of a small figurine depicting a shepherdess sitting on a log with a sheepdog at her feet looking with devotion at his mistress. *A bit like George,* Brenda couldn't help but think.

George sprang to attention. He fumbled under the counter to produce a bunch of keys of which, after a few painful minutes, he selected one. He bounced over to the cabinet to open it, carefully extracted the ornament in question, turning it over for inspection. "Erm, no, it is a Nao," he confirmed apologetically.

Miss Perfect smiled benevolently, "Oh, well, never mind. I only collect the real thing. I don't suppose you have any in the back room, do you?" she asked George, who was returning the shepherdess to her position in the cabinet.

"I'll just lock this up and have a look for you," he replied scuttling off with, Brenda thought, *A bit too much eagerness.* He entered the back room at the same time as Alan was appearing with a tray of tea and biscuits. The two crashed into each other, sending hot tea, mugs, a bowl of sugar lumps and custard creams all over the floor and, to Brenda's secret amusement, splashing the pristine jeans of 'Miss Perfect'.

"Watch where you're going! You nearly bleeding knocked me over," complained Alan. "You nearly gave me an 'eart attack!" he added, "you'd better clear this mess up quick, Health and Safety and all that. You all right, missus?" he addressed the doubled-up figure of 'Miss Perfect' who was attempting to dab tea off her jeans with an inadequate tissue. She was red in the face and quite flustered, Brenda observed. She had lost her poise.

"No, I am not all right, these are expensive trousers bought in Paris. Dry clean only. I cannot meet my friends looking like this," she was almost tearful.

A bit over the top, Brenda thought.

George was beside himself with embarrassment. Scratching his head double time, he paced back and forth, looking for some kind of solution to the problem. At this point, alerted by all the noise, Queenie appeared finishing off what looked like a sausage roll, then wiping her hands on her plastic apron, surveyed the carnage.

"What the 'ell is going on here?" she proclaimed, "I leave you lot for 'alf an 'our and you wreck the shop and pour tea over a punter!" She summed up 'Miss Perfect's' attempts to clean herself up. "It's only tea, love, soak 'em when you get home and wash 'em with a bit of Vanish. Always does the trick." Brushing away the pastry crumbs from around her mouth she observed the two men. "Well, don't just stand there, get a mop and bucket and mop up the mess. We don't want 'ealth and safety issues. It was bad enough when that octogenarian slipped on that melting ice lolly in the summer holidays. What a fuss that was. Threatened to go to the papers and everything. In the end, he settled for a thick winter coat, pork pie 'at and a muffler. We haven't seen 'im since. Wouldn't surprise me if he dropped the lolly there himself."

"Erm," George attempted to interrupt Queenie's tirade, "the lady wondered if we had any pieces of Lladro in the back?"

"What, them building bricks for kiddies? Haven't seen any of that for a long time. I could have a quick scout through the children's toys though, might find something."

Brenda had been observing all of this but felt she ought to clarify what Lladro was to Queenie rather than let her waste her time on searching for the wrong thing.

"I erm," she tentatively began, "I think the lady said Lladro, not Lego – it would be very difficult to build with Lladro. It is a famous pottery and…" she trailed off, realising that everyone had gone silent. George was looking positively scared and Alan had suddenly found a job to do at the other end of the shop. Miss Perfect, sensing the atmosphere, was returning the tissues to her bag and preparing her escape, which she did with far less poise than her entrance. Brenda would probably have been pleased about this if it hadn't been for the fact that Queenie was facing her directly, with her hands placed firmly on her hips.

"I knew that, thank you, I'll 'ave you know I haven't worked for over ten years 'ere without learning a thing or two about pottery. It's just my hearing ain't what it was."

"An easy mistake to make," Brenda retorted apologetically, "I am always mis-hearing things, only the other day I…"

"Well, now that's all sorted, we better get on. George and Alan, ain't you got that mop yet?" Both men hurried into the backroom, glad to escape Queenie's presence for a while. "You getting off soon then?" she asked Brenda, "Linda should be in at one o'clock. Mind you, she has had an 'ell of a lot of time off her shifts because of her treatments. Alan stands in for 'er. He ain't got a lot else to do now he is on his own."

"Well, actually, neither have I," Brenda confessed, "I am awaiting the freeholder of my property to arrive with a spare set of keys to enable me to access my flat. That will not be until after closing, so if it is okay, I would like to stay and help. I could do some sorting of bags if that would fit in with everyone else. If not, I suppose I could always go and sit in the library and read. I am halfway through an Ian McEwan novel so I could pick up where I left off." Brenda was actually starting to feel that might be the better option, bearing in mind what had just happened. She was also reminded of the pangs of hunger in her stomach and knew she was not going to last the afternoon whether that was in the shop or in the library.

At that very moment, George reappeared with a paper bag in his hand, followed by Alan with the requested mop. "I nearly forgot about this, Brenda," he gushed, "Mother was worried about you after I told her the story of your mishap. She got me to make you a couple of cheese and tomato sandwiches. With some Branston pickle," he added with pride. He handed over the bag and turned to help Alan who was looking enviously at the sandwiches.

Brenda could have kissed him, "What a lovely thought. Please thank your mother for me, George." She just about refrained from tearing the package open immediately and consuming the contents without further ado when something about Alan's doleful expression made her feel guilty enough to say, "Alan, I am sure two sandwiches will be far too much for me to eat. Would you like one of them?"

If Brenda had offered him the lottery winnings, Alan could not have been more grateful and on George's instructions, they were allowed to sit together in the back room and share George's cheese and tomato sandwiches, with, of course, pickle that Alan described as the 'cherry on the cake'.

Alan had got up to make them a cup of tea. Whilst the kettle was boiling, he fished in the cupboard for a tin of the 'proper stuff' with a label stating 'Alan' in black marker pen on the side of it. He then produced a small blue teapot, two cups, two teaspoons and a milk jug. He then carefully measured two scoops of tea into the pot, poured on the water and left the tea to brew. He took the milk out of the fridge, sniffed at it suspiciously and satisfied, he poured a measure into the mug. He then put everything on a tray and returned to the slightly incredulous Brenda.

"Learnt to do it properly in the army," he explained, "that and how to smoke and swear were all the skills I came out with. Wished I had never started on the baccy though," he lamented, going into a spasm of coughs as if to prove the point, "my wife said they would be the end of me, then she went first, not right, not right at all." Brenda was about to offer some form of consolation when Alan, calculating the tea was ready, poured out two cups leaving enough room for Brenda to add her own milk. He then sought out two plates from the cupboard and handed Brenda one, looking expectantly at the packet of sandwiches that Brenda had been clutching. She, taking the hint, divided up the contents and for a while they silently ate, enjoying the moment. Then, having finished both his tea and sandwich, Alan brushed the crumbs off his lap and piled up his cup, plate and saucer.

"Finished?" he asked Brenda, who had been so hungry she had demolished hers in indecent haste, nodded and piled up her pottery in the same fashion, handing them to Alan. He took them and proceeded to fill the sink with water, add the washing-up liquid and washed them all up, leaving them to drain in the pink, plastic drainer. Brenda couldn't help but think that this must have been a donation. Who would want a pink, plastic drainer? She rose from her seat, conceding that her breaktime was finished and she must return to the fray.

"I'll go and see what I am needed for," Brenda explained as she headed for the door, "I can be the extra pair of hands this afternoon, I will probably be sorting stock. Are you coming through yet, Alan?"

"Be through in a minute, just catching my breath," Alan wheezed. "Not as young as I used to be," he explained. Brenda halted for a moment, wondering if she ought to stay and see if he was all right. "Go on," he continued, keeping his back to Brenda, "don't want them thinking we are taking too long on our break."

Brenda returned to the shop. George was pacing restlessly, scratching his head and looking around the shop as if searching for an answer to something. Queenie was engaged in conversation with an elderly gentleman who was standing, erect and attentive at the till. The sunken lights in the ceiling had the unfortunate effect of reflecting quite dramatically off his shiny bald head, giving him the appearance of a lighthouse beacon.

"I often go in there," Queenie was in full swing, "best deals I think are the Weatherspoons' All Day Breakfasts. A real bargain and you can have as much coffee as you like. I've been known to stay there all morning with my friend 'elen, putting the world to rights. 'Course we have had other dishes there as well. Fish and chips are nice and they do good puddings." She continued, savouring the memories of other feasts, "Ain't at all expensive, once I…"

"Well, actually," the gentleman interrupted, looking rather puzzled, "I was after the latest Bill Bryson novel, erm, thank you anyway," he spluttered, exiting the premises faster than his age determined, leaving a speechless Queenie, mouth open staring at the door the gentleman had escaped through.

"What's 'e going on about?" she asked the others.

Brenda suddenly clicked the misunderstanding. She giggled and at first couldn't respond.

"What's so funny?" Queenie asked.

"I think the gentleman was enquiring about Waterstones, the book shop, not Wetherspoons the pub," Brenda explained, finding it hard to control her desire to burst into laughter, "an easy mistake to make." She quickly added glancing at George who was still walking tentatively around the shop staring at the ceiling, oblivious to the conversation that had just ensued. Brenda was already regretting her interference, yet again, in Queenie's malapropisms.

Queenie stood still for a moment then suddenly burst into gales of laughter, bending at the middle with the exertion of it. Brenda joined in and George, at last, left off his examination of the ceiling and joined the two women.

"Waterstones, Wetherspoons, oh, my life, what am I like," Queenie managed to get out between the laughter, "'e must 'ave thought I was off me 'ead!" She wiped away tears of laughter from her eyes. "What's up with you, George, you look as if you've seen a ghost?"

"I, er don't want to worry either of you," George responded with considerable head scratching, "but have either of you noticed a dripping of water from the ceiling?"

Brenda certainly hadn't, but both she and Queenie obediently examined the area in question and on cue a few drips landed on Queenie who exclaimed accordingly.

"Bleeding 'ell! What's that all about? We ain't in for another flood like we had in the millennium when that young volunteer got tipsy on Ginger Ale and left the tap running into the sink with the plug in. Right 'how de do' that was. Took ages for the carpet to dry out and we lost a load of jigsaws that were piled in a corner, all the shoes on the shoe rack and the smell didn't go for weeks."

George remained staring at the ceiling. Brenda felt she would try and throw light on the subject. "Who resides above the shop?" she asked, aware that the dripping was becoming more obvious.

"If you mean who lives up there," Queenie responded, "no one, it's a dentist's surgery. Cohen, Bernstein and Shapiro. Been there for years. I've been to them since I started here then my kids and now their kids. I have Mr Cohen, lovely man. He must be in his eighties now but 'e's got no intention of retiring. Good for 'im I says."

"Hadn't we better go upstairs and investigate the source of the water leakage?" Brenda tentatively suggested, receiving a splash in her eye. She noticed there was now an expanding wet patch on the ceiling above the cookery book shelves. If this went on too long, it would bring the ceiling down. "Have we got a bucket we could place under the dripping water? That would at least spare the floor from getting too wet?" Brenda hoped she wasn't being too bossy, especially as this was only the second day she had worked in the shop. However, on her instructions, George sprang into action, rushing with some urgency into the back room, reappearing with the bucket and Alan, who had obviously been napping in the back after his lunch but was now fully awake and 'on the case'.

"Turn all the lights off," he commanded, "the water might get into the electrics. Then we will have a problem. Don't want anyone getting electrocuted. Has anyone thought of going upstairs and telling Mr Cohen?"

"Well. I…" Brenda began but Alan was already heading towards the front door. The water was now getting quite persistent and the bucket was filling up. George was rushing in and out with spare buckets, lining them up to catch the various sources of the leaks, then pushing rails away from the wet areas. The few customers who had remained in the shop, more to watch the potential catastrophe than to purchase any item, decided to leave after the warning of electrocution. The shop was now empty, so that gave George plenty of room to shuffle items about, take some into the back room and generally reorganise.

Queenie, who, up to now, had been more of an observer, stirred herself. "'s 'appened before. He won't spend the money on new pipes or a plumber, come to that. Got 'is nephew in last time to patch it all up. Must be about the fourth time this has happened since last Christmas. It will happen at night when no one is 'ere. Then we will be 'aving to make ourselves a flippin' ark like Noah to get out of 'ere," she chuckled to herself, "I says to him, Mr Cohen, what are you saving your money for; you can't take it 'wiv' you. 'Queenie,' he says, 'the Pharaohs did, why not me?' He has a sense of humour, that one. Lovely man, our Mr Cohen."

Brenda was getting quite worried about the situation. There were obviously not enough buckets to cope with the flow of water which was increasing in intensity. Brenda envisaged the ceiling coming down at any minute. "Do you think we ought to ring the fire brigade?" she suggested to George whose head scratching and pacing had now got quite manic. It struck her how vulnerable he was and how completely out of his comfort zone. He really did not know how to handle this sort of emergency. She put her hand on his arm to slow him down. "George, did you hear me?"

"What? Er, what did you say?"

"I suggested calling the fire brigade, the water is getting out of hand and I wouldn't like to see the ceiling coming down. Shall I use your phone or the store phone to do it?" Brenda asked, watching the flow of water reach the entrance door. Then, to see in horror two elderly woman entering the premises, completely unperturbed by the water or the obvious disarray of the shop contents, and paddled their way to the till clutching a well-used Iceland carrier bag, from where one of them pulled out an Arran jumper that looked as if it had seen better days. Queenie, who had been leaning over the counter, watching the water proceedings, stood up and looked at the item before her. Brenda felt this was going to be a clash of the Titans.

"I bought this jumper in here and I followed the washing instructions and it has shrunk. I want my money back. Don't ask me if I want anything else instead, because I don't. I come in here enough to know what you've got and haven't got, so money back if you don't mind," she barked, glaring at Queenie from under her tightly pulled down, blue rain hat. Her friend, of similar stature and demeanour, was backing her up in a rear-guard action behind her left shoulder.

Queenie pulled herself up to her full height and examined the jumper closely, looking inside the collar, Brenda assumed for washing instructions, holding the article up to the light and measuring it against her own body. She sniffed, hummed and rubbed her chin and then posed the ultimate question, "Do you have the receipt? No refunds without a receipt."

"I don't tend to keep receipts from charity shops."

"Well, how long ago did yer buy it then? We allow twenty-eight days to return it for a money refund, after that you have to exchange it, but if you ain't got the receipt then there is nothing I can do about it. Looks like you've had plenty of wear outa' this. Don't even remember seeing it in the shop and I'm 'ere most days," Queenie sniffed again.

Brenda was amazed that this conversation was ensuing as water was now forming a rivulet down the centre of the shop chased by George who had found an inadequate mop to attempt to soak some of it up. Both women seemed oblivious, as did Queenie. Brenda had images of them floating out into the High Street still continuing with the dialogue.

"When did I buy it, Mollie?" the customer addressed her friend, "cannot be more than two months ago, can it. You would have thought a charity shop would be a bit more sympathetic and automatically give me my money back with no questions asked."

"Oh, more like two years ago," Mollie naively replied, "I know because it was about the time my Jamie came back from Birmingham to settle in London. We came…" she was cut off by her friend who was glaring at her and shaking her head. "Oh, maybe it was less than that, my memory isn't what it was," she continued unconvincingly.

The water was now dripping on all three of the women at the till. If Queenie noticed it, Brenda mused, then she was not going to let a little thing like wet hair distract her from her purpose. The lady in the rain hat was well equipped and Brenda would not have been surprised if she had not unfurled the umbrella she had protruding from her raincoat pocket, if not to shelter from the ever-increasing water flow, but also as a weapon against Queenie.

Just as Brenda was about to abandon ship, retreat to the back room and ring the fire brigade until order of some sort had been restored, Alan appeared from his sojourn upstairs, looking triumphant. He was met though with a scream from Molly who, having not had the protection of a hat, had plucked an object from her hair that had dropped on her from the ceiling.

"A tooth!" she cried. At which point, the argument at the till ceased.

Chapter 6

Brenda had returned to her flat at the appointed time and met the freeholder to collect the spare key to enable her to gain access. The relief at being able to have a long soak in the bath, have a proper dinner sitting in front of the television, catching up on a couple of soaps she had recorded, felt like bliss. She had located her spare door and car keys and dug out another handbag and was able to forage another set of contents for it.

The morning after her return, she went down to the shops to buy her groceries and as a last-minute addition, popped in a prawn pasta and salad layer; just as a memory of the night on the shop floor. She then returned to a modest lunch and did a bit of housework. She opened the three letters that had arrived: a brochure from Saga Holidays, a flyer from the local theatre about the Christmas Pantomime and reminder from the chiropodist of her next appointment. It was now two o'clock and Brenda was bored. She wondered what the matter was with her. She didn't usually mind a free afternoon to catch up on a bit of reading or to indulge herself in a film on the television. Sometimes, she had been known to drive to the cinema and see a film on the big screen. She didn't mind doing things on her own. As an only child, she had got used to it. Then as an adult, she had never been particularly gregarious, her work colleagues remained as such and she did not meet them outside the confines of the office walls, except for Christmas and leaving events. Now and then, someone would drift into her life, but then disappear for whatever reason. There had been a man friend once. He was called Derek and she had met him on a singles holiday she had gone on when she turned forty. His wife had died very young in a car crash, which he survived. It seemed to Brenda that he had not really forgiven himself for getting out alive when she was killed. He had a large portrait of her hanging over his fireplace with a set of three candles under it, which he lit every night. He bought fresh flowers every week to place in a tall, glass vase to the side of the portrait; always red roses as she apparently came from Lancashire and he wanted something symbolic. He was a charming man and took Brenda to the opera and theatre in London, but she knew she would never be able to compete with his first true love. It all ended abruptly when Derek announced that one of his two daughters, who had been very close to his wife, did not like her father 'dating' someone else and said he had to choose between Brenda or her. No contest.

So, here she was on her own again, but now not happy with it. The bustle of the shop, the traumas that had occurred, the conversations she had had with the other volunteers, George and his head scratching, the customers, she realised, had wakened up something in her to meet more people and to perhaps do more than one day in the Charity Shop?

No sooner than the idea had come into her head she had donned her coat, gathered her spare handbag put on another pair of shoes, (the other ones were still drying out from the flood), grabbed her spare keys and was down the stairs before she could change her mind. She enjoyed her walk to the shop; she was driving less and less since her retirement. She felt it did her good. She didn't want to join a gym, paying ridiculous fees and sweating on a treadmill surrounded by conspicuously fit twenty-year olds with stomachs like planks, tight bottoms and defined calves. She couldn't really picture herself in Lycra either. So, she stuck to walking and the odd swim at the local council-run Sports centre. She avoided the times the children would be swimming, splashing everyone and screaming as they jumped in the deep end.

It didn't take her long to get to the Charity Shop. She wasn't sure what she was going to say or if the shop would even be open after the flood. When she had left, there had been major problems. They were wary of turning on the lights and hadn't located an electrician who could come immediately. However, she was pleased to see the door was open and people were leaving and entering. The floor looked a lot dryer and Alan was happily standing behind the till, which had been cleared of all its rubbish that had got soaked, and looked quite neat and tidy. He was taking a carrier bag from a customer who then left, pushing Brenda out of the way rudely before walking briskly up the road.

"Hello, everyone," Brenda called out, "I'm a glutton for punishment, you just can't get rid of me." This was met with silence so she tried again. "Did the leak from upstairs get sorted out?"

Alan looked up from the carrier bag he was sorting out. "What did you say? Hearing's not what it was. Could you take over the till whilst I sort this problem out?" he shouted behind him as he rushed into the back room with the bag that was obviously causing him a lot of soul searching. Eagerly Brenda took up her position behind the till, glad to be back in the fray. Five minutes later, Alan emerged with George in tow, worriedly scratching his head. He approached Brenda.

"Brenda, did you take a good look at the customer who brought in the carrier bag?"

"I was too worried about him knocking me over in his indecent haste to exit the premises to take note of his inside leg measurements. Why, what has he done? Is he a terrorist…" joked Brenda, but was cut off mid-sentence by the piercing sound of a police siren which she thought was just coincidental until two burly policeman carrying walkie talkies entered the shop and started looking around the rails, back room and toilet etc.

George was hyperventilating by now. Alan was still holding on to the carrier bag but seemed to be frozen to the spot. George at last extracted the bag from Alan and waved it at the policeman like a white flag. "I think this is maybe what you are looking for," he squeaked, "a gentleman brought it in about ten minutes ago but rushed out quickly and according to my colleague, disappeared up the High Street in the direction of Laura Ashley. We did look inside it and found a considerable amount of presumably illegal substances and packs of needles."

"I recognised it straight away from years of watching Crime Watch," chipped in Alan, "worth a fortune, this little lot."

Brenda was too shocked to speak. *Who would deposit drugs in a charity shop?* It seemed the most unlikely of places, but then again that was probably the very reason he did it. Brenda wanted excitement in her life, but she had not bargained for this.

One of the policemen took the bag from Alan, "Yes, this is what we were after. Who actually saw what he looked like?"

Brenda blushed, feeling guilty for not being more observant, but she needn't have worried as Alan was attempting a somewhat general description of the man who Brenda could only assume was a drug dealer. The policeman made some notes, "Did any of you touch the contents?"

Now it was Alan's turn to look embarrassed as George and Brenda denied handling the bag at all. Alan had to admit he had taken one of the packets out of the bag to identify what it was.

"You will have to accompany me down to the police station to have your fingerprints taken to eliminate them from the identification of the owner of the bag," the policeman explained.

Alan already had his coat on and was ready to go. Brenda suspected he was looking forward to a ride in a police car, especially if the siren was turned on. The other policeman had been talking into his Walkie Talkie and relayed information to his colleague, then ran out in the same direction the drug dealer had gone. Alan was accompanied to the car, the policeman turned it around and with a squeal of tyres and sped off down the High Street.

Brenda hoped Alan had remembered to 'clunk click every trip' and wear his seat belt.

It seemed very quiet after they had left. Luckily, no customers had been involved and Queenie had missed it all, as it was her day off. George was completely out of his comfort zone, Brenda thought. "What about I put the kettle on and we have a nice cup of tea," Brenda suggested. George seemed to brighten up a little bit at the thought of liquid refreshment but something was obviously on his mind.

"Do you think the dealer will be back for his carrier bag if he thinks the coast is clear?"

Admittedly, Brenda had not thought of this, but in an attempt to calm George's fears, she assured him that he would be caught before that happened but it was probably a good idea to close the shop anyway.

So, earlier than usual, the shop door was shut, the open sign turned around to become closed, and Brenda and George retreated to the sanctuary of the back to drink tea and consume rather more custard creams than usual on the grounds they needed the sugar for shock.

Chapter 7

Brenda decided to return to her flat, having walked part of the way with George. They had assumed that Alan had gone home after his trip to the police station as he still had not returned to the shop before they closed. Brenda had suggested she should go in the next day as Alan may not put in an appearance after his ordeal. George, hardly listening, had agreed so they said their farewells at the corner by the Tattoo Parlour and Brenda continued her journey on her own. She hadn't gone very far when she was aware that she was being followed. Cold fear gripped her as she thought of the drug dealer and the hoard he left behind him. A hand touched her elbow and a high, childish voice, certainly not belonging to the gruff man she bumped into, whispered at her.

"Are you the lady what works in the Charity Shop on the 'igh Street?"

Brenda turned around and recognised the voice as to belonging to one of the 'Horrible Teenagers' she presumed had stolen her handbag.

"I am," she replied.

"I've got yer bag. It ain't got the money in it cos we spent that – there weren't a lot anyways – but I didn't think it were right that you should lose yer bag, like, cos I wouldn't like losing all my stuff," she rambled on at an alarming pace, "so I wanted te 'ave it back like, even though Sophie told us to chuck it, I made out, like, that I were going to throw it in one of them big bin things outside of Tesco but I stuffed it up me jumper and took it home. I were worried, like, that me mum would clock on, but I hid it under me bed. She weren't none the wiser, not that she could give a sh…"

Brenda cut her off, worried that she would go on like this forever. "I'm not going to pretend that I'm not annoyed with you for stealing my handbag in the first place," she paused, "but thank you, nevertheless, for returning it, albeit minus the twenty-five pounds sixty. I should really ring the police, but I hope you have learnt a lesson from this whole unfortunate incident?"

The girl looked rather bemused and rubbed her nose with the back of her hand. "I don't want no lecture, just wanted you to 'ave yer stuff back. See yer," she called out as she swung around on her inappropriately high heels and strutted up the road. Brenda stood watching her for a while, then, turned to continue her journey home, but something made her turn around. The girl had stopped and was standing alone, trying to light the end of a cigarette, her hand cupped around it in an attempt to prevent the wind blowing it out. She looked so young and vulnerable. Brenda realised it must have taken a lot of guts to bring the bag back to her, risking the condemnation of her friends if they found out. The girl, having achieved her aim, set off again, disappearing around a corner and out of view.

When she arrived back at the flat and let herself in, she emptied out the contents of the returned handbag. The girl had been telling the truth. Only the money had gone, everything else they had not bothered with. Somehow, Brenda felt the bag was rather tainted now and she threw it into the bin along with the half-eaten mints and cereal bar. She cut up the old cards she had now replaced, but everything else she reassigned to her replacement bag. Still quite incredulous about the whole encounter, she put on the kettle. It was then she realised there was a folded-up sheet of A4 paper pushed through her letter box, lying on the mat. She rescued it and read the neatly written note.

'Dear Miss Watts,

I hope all is well after your unfortunate set of circumstances. I am glad I could be of some help. However, it is my turn to ask a favour of you. The monthly Residents' Meeting should have been held at number fifteen but Mrs Kershaw has had to go up to Bishop Stortford's to help out with the grandchildren whilst her daughter goes into hospital for a minor operation. I wondered if you would be so kind as to hold the meeting at your flat instead. I would offer, but my wife has not been at all well this past week.

Yours faithfully,

Richard Draycotte.'

Brenda stared at the note for a while. She had managed to avoid hosting these events up to now, relying on those who loved to be in charge. *Oh well*, she thought, *first time for everything.*

The monthly meeting was always the fourth Thursday of the month starting at seven-thirty, to allow those tenants who worked to get home and have their dinner, and usually finished at ten o'clock after a cup of tea or coffee and a biscuit. She glanced at her calendar and realised that was tomorrow. Brenda, suddenly feeling flustered, made a mental note to buy a couple of packets of M&S biscuits for the occasion and perhaps another jar of Nescafe as the one she had in the cupboard had solidified from age and lack of use. Then a thought struck her, had Richard informed the other tenants of the changed venue? She looked at her watch, five thirty. He would probably be in, preparing the dinner, so she hastily grabbed her keys and descended the stairs to Richard's flat.

Knocking at Richard's door produced no response, so she tried the doorbell. There was a considerable pause and Brenda was about to leave when the door opened a couple of inches and Richard's head appeared. "Yes?" he enquired, looking none too pleased at the sight of Brenda, clutching her keys and the creased note he had written to her. "Have you come to tell me you can't do the meeting?"

"No, no," Brenda reassured him, "I just wondered if you had informed the others the meeting was at my flat?"

Richard looked puzzled for a moment and strain showed on his lined face and Brenda felt there was something very wrong. "Are you all right, Richard, is there anything I can do to help?" she ventured.

"It's Maureen, she has taken a turn for the worse, I can't get a word out of her and she won't eat a thing. I can't even tempt her with her Heinz tomato soup and she loves that, especially on a cold day. I..." he trailed off, still standing with the door partially closed and his head protruding from the gap. Brenda couldn't see inside the room but she could tell the curtains were closed and the smell of stale cooking and, surprisingly, cigarette smoke hit her nostrils.

"Would you like me to call the doctor or help you by doing some shopping or tidying around or..."

"No, thanks, I am perfectly capable of looking after my own wife, thank you very much. You are just like Social Services, poking their noses in where they are not wanted." With that, Brenda found the door slammed in her face and still the question of the information about the changed venue had not been answered.

Brenda stood for a moment, surprised at this generally mild man's behaviour. *Still, there is nothing I can do,* she thought to herself as she returned to her own flat feeling quite deflated. She decided to have a cup of tea before preparing her dinner and perhaps catching up on the news at Six on the T.V. Maybe she would have a couple of squares of dark chocolate that she kept for occasions of stress, which she felt the day's events justified. She was just pouring the tea into her favourite bone china mug, thinking about the drug dealer and the girl who returned her handbag, the Charity Shop and Richard and his ill wife when she had a moment of realisation. Her life was changing, she was no longer bored and feeling she had no purpose in life. Since her voluntary work had begun, her days were filled with excitement and interest. She wondered where it would all lead.

Taking an extra square of chocolate and her tea, she sat down to listen to the news that seemed much tamer than her own life. Brenda giggled to herself then settled back into her chair allowing herself the luxury of a quick nap before dinner and then watching some television.

It must have been about eight o' clock when Brenda heard the telephone ring out loudly against the monotonous tones of a so-called celebrity describing the interior of a stately home somewhere in Cheshire. She hadn't really wanted to watch it but she had finished her Victoria Hislop from the library and had little else to do. She leant over to answer it, nearly knocking over the cup of cold tea she had not finished earlier.

"Oh, Brenda," a familiar voice came over the line. "It's George. Linda isn't well again. I know it's short notice but could you fill in for her tomorrow afternoon? There will be you, Queenie and myself. Alan is doing the morning shift but he is off at two. Will that be okay? Don't worry if you can't, we can manage. We could have no…"

Brenda interrupted him, feeling his anxiety over the phone, "It would be a pleasure, George, I will see you tomorrow."

Brenda replaced the receiver, feeling a warmth of contentment at being wanted. An emotion she had rarely felt in her life. Even when her mother became reliant on her for all her needs, Brenda felt her mother thought it was a daughter's duty and she rarely got a please or thank you. At work, she was just part of the furniture, reliable but replaceable. Forgotten about immediately after her retirement, probably before she had crossed the road to catch her bus on her last day in the office. Brenda chastised herself for wallowing in self-pity and focused on collecting together what she would need for the next day's afternoon shift. If she went early, she could pop into M&S first for the biscuits, have a bite to eat in the 'Cosy Corner Café' on Bridge Street then go on to the Charity Shop. Satisfied she had everything organised, she focused on making her evening meal and then got an early night.

Chapter 8

The next day, Brenda checked the alarm was on and securing her door she descended the stairs, pausing briefly outside Richard and Maureen's flat, remembering the rather strange encounter she had experienced yesterday. Perhaps she should knock and see if everything was all right? Then again, she didn't want to interfere – no, she would leave it and perhaps call around this evening before the meeting.

It was quite a pleasant day and Brenda enjoyed her walk. *Nice bit of fresh air, clear the lungs*, she told herself. Often with the central heating on, Brenda's tiny flat could feel quite stuffy. She reached M&S and descended to the Food Hall. She bought two packets of biscuits, a jar of decaf coffee and a packet of sugar. Not many people tended to have sugar in their drinks now, but you never know. She tried to remember what her role should be if she was housing the meeting. She supposed it was just to provide the refreshments and the chairs to sit on. *Chairs,* thought Brenda, *have I enough chairs*? She counted in her head the number of residents that normally attended the meeting, minus Richard, then totalled the number of chairs she had, including two fold-up portable ones she had for days on the beach at Frinton and realised there was a deficit of three. Why hadn't she thought of that before? It would have been the perfect excuse not to hold the meeting at her house. Still, too late now. She couldn't ask them to sit on the floor, not at their ages. Brenda was one of the youngest occupants who attended the meetings, most of the younger ones were too busy to attend.

By the time Brenda arrived at the shop, after a quick lunch at 'The Cosy Café', she had formulated a plan. She would initially see if there were any fold-up chairs in the back room of the shop and if not, see if she could borrow any from George's or Queenie's. She wondered if that would look presumptuous, but *There's nothing wrong with asking,* she told herself.

Brenda couldn't believe what she was seeing when she arrived at the shop. There was a small crowd of onlookers outside, blocking, at first, an almost surreal sight of a metal signpost that had somehow been hit hard enough to have ended up being thrust through the display window, smashing the glass and devastating the World War Two theme that Queenie had painstakingly created. Books, model airplanes, a helmet, gas mask and a lot of Union Jack flags littered the pavement, rolling about in the wind. George and Queenie were attempting to gather them up with the help, or hinderance of eager onlookers, whose contribution in some cases was to pocket their booty and disappear quickly up the road. Brenda immediately sprang into action, trying to obstruct some of the flying papers and recovering a photo album that was shedding its sepia prints of a family during the Second World War.

"What happened?" Brenda shouted out to a manic George who was trying to collect the escaping items at the same time as stopping customers entering the shop.

"A lorry swerved off the road and hit a lamp post that smashed through our window."

"Bleeding bad luck is all we're gerring at the moment," joined in Queenie, "what wiv the flood and the drug dealer, now this. You couldn't make it up. We'll 'ave to shut this afternoon. Wasted trip for you, Bren."

Brenda had never been called Bren in her life. Her parents had never shortened her name and this had continued throughout her schooling then work. It felt rather good to have a definitive of her name – as if she belonged.

"I wouldn't dream of leaving you with all this mess. I'll stay and help you tidy up. Have the authorities been informed?"

"George has done all that. Ain't that right, George?"

George, satisfied that all that could be salvaged, was now safely back in the shop, had turned to examining the offending lamp post that was forming a barrier across the pavement ending up through the shop window. He tentatively tugged at the post, then quickly changed his mind.

"What was that, Queenie?" he at last replied, scratching his head at the whole dilemma.

"I was saying you had it all sorted. You had rung the police and the shop owners about the obstruction and the damage."

"Yes, shouldn't be too long before they rope the area off and board up the window. I remember a similar occasion a few years ago during a bad winter and a car skidded on black ice and ended up as part of our window display. Took ages to move it. The driver was as right as rain. Just a bit shell shocked. She was a Religious Education teacher at the school around the corner. She was more concerned about being late for registration."

Queenie, by now, had positioned herself in front of the shop window, preventing eager customers from gaining entrance to the shop via the hole in the window. Some had already achieved it and were inside, happily looking around as if getting in through a smashed window was quite the norm. Brenda was amazed.

A van drew up and a couple of men got out with the obvious purpose of securing the area.

"Should I go in and man the till? Or even woman the till?" Brenda joked and then immediately regretted attempting levity at a time like this.

"Thank you, that would be a good idea," George replied whilst attempting to explain the situation to the two overall-clad men who stood, hands on hips shaking their heads and tutting simultaneously. Brenda heard the word tea and then an annoyed Queenie entered the shop muttering something about only having one pair of hands, followed by the kettle being filled and the sound of mugs being slammed on the surface by the sink.

There was a customer clutching a box to her chest by the till, so Brenda went over smiling as if there was nothing untoward about a lamppost through the window. "Hello, can I help you?" Brenda enquired.

"I've just brought in a vase, nothing special. I don't want to throw it away, but I'm moving into a bungalow and I have to get rid of a lot of things as there isn't much room and I don't want to be dusting endlessly at my time of life," she handed over the box, "I will go now as I don't want to be tempted to buy anything else. That's how I bought the vase in the first place. Not from here though. Down the road at the Heart Foundation." With that she left the shop briskly.

Brenda tore off the Sellotape from the box and unwrapped the vase that had been carefully protected with bubble wrap. It was very unusual. She turned it upside down and discovered the label was still on it.

'Rene Lalique
Meandres Vase
c. 1935 France'

Brenda instinctively knew that the vase was valuable. She carefully placed it on the counter and ran to the door to see if the lady was still in view but there was no sign of her. She ran back inside again to retrieve the vase in case a customer should fancy it before they had a chance to value it. Brenda felt quite excited. She hadn't felt like this since she found a man's wallet stuffed with ten-pound notes on the side of a towpath. She had looked inside but there was no address. She took it to a police station and handed it in. She thought she might get a reward for being so honest, but she never heard anything at all from its owner or the police.

"What's up 'wiv' you, Bren?" she heard Queenie ask, "you look like the cat who's got the cream."

"I think we have been left a very valuable vase," gabbled Brenda, "I'm not entirely certain but we could Google it to see what it may be worth."

"I'll come inside 'wiv' 'yer', George can manage out 'ere. It won't take them men long to put up a bit of tape and we can finish the rest later, after we've 'ad a cuppa."

Brenda went ahead to put the kettle on again, secure in the knowledge that George was not allowing any more customers into the shop, on 'Health and Safety' grounds. She got out the mugs and deposited the tea bags in them. As Alan wasn't in yet, she did not bother with the teapot. Queenie had gone straight to her handbag and was emptying out its contents one by one until she located her phone. Then there was a lot of tutting and mumbling as she attempted to operate it, then further mumbling as she retrieved her magnifiers. Satisfied at last, she sat down and proceeded to operate the phone.

"Right, 'ere goes, I'm on Google. What is the make of the vase? Has it gor' a label?"

Brenda dictated the details she had read from the base of the vase and after several corrections of how to spell it she managed to bring up a picture of the vase Brenda was holding with the details and a price.

"Rene Lalique, Meandres Vase, c. 1935, two thousand, two hundred and fifty pounds," Queenie sprung up out of the chair, as fast as her knees would allow, and did a little dance in a circle, grabbing Brenda on one of the rotations so they were dancing together when Alan walked in, early for his afternoon shift.

"What's up with you two? Careful you don't knock that tea over!" he exclaimed.

"Just look what Bren has uncovered. Lady brought it in earlier and she recognised it as being worth summut and it is – it's bleeding worth two thousand, two hundred and fifty pounds!"

Alan looked stunned at this information. "Who brought it in?" he asked, "does she know what it's worth?"

"I tried to catch her but she had disappeared by the time I realised what she had given me," Brenda explained, still feeling rather uneasy about the situation.

"Ain't your fault," interrupted Queenie, "and the money is all for charity. It ain't as if we are going to pocket it ourselves, is it?" Brenda felt a slight note of regret in Queenie's voice but quickly brushed the thought aside.

"I'll get George to take a photograph of the vase on his phone, he's better at it than me. Then we can send it to our eBay hub or even take it to auction?" Brenda suggested.

Alan's ears pricked up at this, "I've never been to an auction, always fancied going. There are auction rooms on Cotswold Street, near the Fire Station. We could go there if you want, Brenda, to see what we could get? Can you find out when they are open, Queenie?"

Queenie was looking none too pleased at being left out of the Auction Room visit but returned to the Google site again and found the auction room's opening times. "Every other Saturday from 10 a.m.," she read, "and there is one this weekend."

"Perfect!" Alan exclaimed, "Police witness yesterday, an auction this Saturday. What next? Is that all right with you, Brenda?"

Brenda contemplated getting out her diary, but she knew perfectly well she was free, as she was most weekends, since the death of her mother. "That is fine, Alan. Shall I meet you there at 9.45?" Brenda always liked to be well in time.

At this point, George appeared looking more frazzled and unkempt than normal. Queenie got up to make him a cup of tea and Alan pulled a chair over for him to sit down.

"You all right?" Queenie enquired, "'ave they boarded up the window yet? Bleeding punters would still be walking in if we had found a bomb in 'ere."

"Yes, all secure now until the glaziers come to put in a new pane of glass. I suppose we will get the money back from the insurance company. They are arriving on Monday. I just hope the boards survive the weekend," He scratched his head and Queenie handed him his tea and a custard cream biscuit, patting him on his shoulder. Brenda could not help but think that Queenie counted George as one of her children, rather than her manager. For all her forthrightness, Queenie had a heart of gold.

Alan filled George in with the details of the vase and his visit to the police station whilst Brenda went out to see for herself the shop, darkened by the boarded window, the smell of wood shavings and an eerie silence interrupted only by George's exclamations as the vase story unfolded.

What a day it had been. Brenda felt quite proud of her detection of the valuable vase and now she had something purposeful to do on Saturday. A morning at the auction rooms. Another new experience in the life of Brenda Watts.

Chapter 9

George had locked up early as there was no point in remaining when the shop was shut for custom. Brenda was happy with this as she had the residents' meeting that night, so she gathered up her carrier bag with the biscuits and coffee and began her journey home. She realised too late that she had completely forgotten to see if she could borrow the three chairs. She was just mentally counting how many chairs she had and worrying that there would not be enough when she saw a familiar figure, huddled up in an inadequate coat, attempting to light a cigarette with matches that kept blowing out. It was the teenager who had returned her bag. Brenda felt sorry for her even though she knew she was a thief, but a thief who had felt guilty enough to return her handbag with all its belongings intact, except the money. She looked so young, lost, cold and vulnerable. Brenda was suddenly compelled to walk over to her. She wasn't sure what she was going to say but the girl looked up and spotted her. Stuffing the unlit cigarette back into its packet she folded her arms against the cold and dashed up the road without looking behind her. *Oh well,* Brenda thought, *she is obviously embarrassed.* So, she continued with her journey back to her flat. She had a lot to do before the meeting started at seven o clock.

Brenda couldn't get the mental picture of the girl out of her mind. She somehow felt responsible for her. She wondered if the other girls, Sophie in particular, had found out about her bag being returned, hence the quick departure of the girl on seeing her. She imagined all the things the girls may have subjected her to: verbal and physical abuse, putting her 'into Coventry' a ploy, girls loved to put their victims through, one she had suffered herself at school, always being an outsider and unpopular with her peers. This brought it all back to Brenda as she returned home contemplating 'man's inhumanity to man'.

Brenda arrived back at the flats. She knocked on Richard's door on her way up the stairs but there was no reply. Perhaps he had taken Maureen to the doctor's, or even the hospital. He had been very worried about her and Brenda was worried about him as well. He had looked awful the other day. *Oh well*, she thought, *none of my business.*

She calculated she would need about thirteen chairs, not an easy task in her tiny front room. She brought out the two folding chairs she had bought for her and her mum to sit on Frinton Beach. Brenda was glad they were coming in useful again. She had a small sofa for two and two separate armchairs and four wooden chairs that sat around her small pine dining table. Ten in total. She calculated that with some residents hardly ever attending, it would be a squeeze but they would manage. Lucky, in a way that Mrs Kershaw couldn't come and she doubted Richard would turn up. Of the other flats, Brenda knew three were unoccupied, five were holiday lets and the others were occupied by young city workers who would not be home on time for the meeting and had no interest in attending anyway.

Bill arrived first. He chose a comfy seat and sat quietly eyeing up the biscuits, answering Brenda's polite questions about his health and holidays etc. with monosyllabic replies. She was glad when Pat and her neighbour, whose name Brenda could never remember, arrived. Pat was the source of all information about the residents of the flats. Brenda had learnt very quickly to have an excuse at the ready if she met Pat on the stairs. She had been known to trap Brenda for half an hour, enlightening her on some scandal associated with the other residents, probably embellished with considerable poetic license. However, tonight she was a welcome voice who would fill in the conversation gaps until everyone arrived.

The rest arrived in rapid succession after that. Leonard from number two, Winston from number twenty-five, Sheila from number eighteen, Fatima from number eight, Kayleigh from number nineteen and finally, and late as always, David from number twenty-four (train got stuck between two stations, took them ages to sort it out). The coffee and tea preferences were sorted out and with the help of Pat and her friend they were distributed accordingly. Whilst everyone was happily chomping at Brenda's posh biscuits, except for Fatima who was going to weight-watchers after the meeting, Brenda went through the minutes of the last meeting that Richard had posted through her door soon after having asked her to house the occasion. Everyone nodded their agreement of the points and so, using the order in which the minutes listed them, Brenda started the usual list of points to be discussed. Most of it was routine. The main point of contention, and had been since Brenda moved in, was the painting of the exterior of the property which continued to get more and more discoloured and tatty. What used to be white was now a grimy grey and Brenda was convinced this put potential tenants off, hence the two unoccupied flats.

Leonard said he would write again to Mr Patel and see if he could convince him to employ someone to brighten the place up. Bin collection was discussed and the upkeep of the garden. Both were inadequately executed and the perusal of this was left to Bill and Sheila respectively. It was in 'Any Other Business' that Brenda piped up.

"Has anyone seen Richard from number fourteen recently? I am very worried about him. He was so stressed about his wife's health the last time I saw him and now he just isn't answering his door." There were mumbles of agreement and Pat and her friend said that he always used to have a chat with them on the staircase.

"Did you all know his wife, Maureen, is in a wheelchair and he has to feed her and do everything for her?" Brenda asked

"I did," Winston responded, "but only because I work at St Luke's Hospital and Richard brings Maureen up for her consultations every two weeks. She is a very ill lady. I am sometimes working in that clinic when they come for the appointment. Thinking about it, I haven't seen them for a while." He frowned and rubbed his eyes. Winston was a serious young man who worked double shifts and always seemed tired. "I'll try and see if they know anything about it at the hospital and I'll try knocking at their door after the meeting."

"I'll come with you, Winston," Brenda chipped in. "If that is okay with you?" she quickly added.

"That will be fine," Winston replied, downing the last dregs of his black coffee with a half teaspoon of sugar. Brenda was glad she had replenished the sugar bowl with brown demerara and she had kept her fingers crossed that no one would want it in their tea. She had been lucky.

The meeting came to an end soon after that and Pat and her friend helped Brenda clear away the cups, saucers and biscuit plates. Brenda noted the absence of any surplus biscuits and wondered if she had not supplied a sufficient amount. *Oh well, too late to worry about that now.* They had agreed on a date for the next meeting which would be held at Sheila's who would inform Mrs Kershaw and the other two who were unable to make tonight's meeting. Brenda said she would tell Richard tonight or push a note through his door.

Winston helped her fold up the garden chairs and generally clear around. Brenda noticed how tidy he was as he straightened coasters and realigned the settee with the marks on the floor where it had originally been positioned. He was a handsome young man, Brenda thought to herself. Quiet and unassuming, he seemed to work all around the clock and when he was at home he never seemed to have visitors. He was on the same floor as her and Brenda was never aware of any noise or music emanating from number twenty-five. That was not to say he didn't have friends or a girlfriend. He probably met them outside the vicinity of the flat, keeping his social life private. Brenda could understand that. She was a very private person and never discussed her social life, what there had been of it, even with her mother.

She remembered being routinely cross-examined after she had been to an office party or had accepted an invitation to the cinema or a meal, which wasn't often. She had learned to be economical with the truth, just allowing her mother enough information to keep her happy.

Brenda locked up and she accompanied Winston down the stairs to Richard and Maureen's flat. Winston rang the bell and waited. There was no reply. Brenda suggested knocking as well in case the doorbell wasn't working. This had happened to Brenda on several occasions. The bells were cheap and unreliable. She had kept meaning to invest in a new and more efficient one. However, she had learnt it was a wonderful excuse to leave the door firmly closed on unwelcome guests. Still there was no response from Richard. They were about to concede defeat when the door opened a crack and Richards head appeared. He looked terrible. His hair was unbrushed and his face was as white as a sheet, contrasted with the dark lines under his staring, vacant eyes.

"Hi, Richard," Winston began, "Brenda and I were just wondering how Maureen was and whether there was anything we could do? Anything you needed from the shops?"

Richard stared at him blankly.

"If it's an inconvenient time, we could come back," Winston continued.

Then, suddenly, Richard started to cry. The sobbing was coming from deep within him, shaking his whole body as the tears streamed down his face. He let go of the door handle and covered his eyes with his hands trying to speak at the same time but the words were distorted with anguish. Brenda stepped forward and put her arms around the man she had always known to be in control, organised, efficient and on top of things. She hardly recognised this wrecked version of the original and just wanted to put it all right for him. She was normally very unresponsive, the opposite to 'touchy feely'. However, the plight of her neighbour had brought out another side to Brenda. She offered soothing words to Richard, rocking him in her arms like a baby.

Winston, meanwhile, had been sniffing the air. He had a frown on his face and a worried look in his eyes. "Is it okay, Richard, if I say hello to Maureen?" he ventured.

There was no reply from Richard, so Winston entered the flat. Brenda remained with Richard; she was filled with foreboding – something was not right but she did not even want to start guessing what it was. Slowly, Richard stopped crying and Brenda was able to release her arms and steer him back into the flat. She was hit by the indescribable stench. However, their progress was halted by Winston. He gently took Richard by the hand and led him to a chair in the tiny kitchen.

"How long has Maureen been dead, Richard?"

Richard looked blank. His bottom lip trembled and Brenda thought he was going to start crying again and searched out a strip of kitchen roll she found beside the toaster. However, Richard had by now gained some control of his emotions and replied quietly but assuredly, "A few days? A week? I've lost track of time. She wanted to do it on her birthday, but I wouldn't let her. I wanted us to spend one more birthday together. I didn't know what to do you see. She had it all planned for a long time. She was saving up her sleeping tablets, putting them down the side of the seat of her wheelchair. I should have got rid of them, I knew she was doing it. She knew that soon she would lose the ability to swallow so she had to do it fairly quickly. I told her it was wrong. That she should wait for nature's end. She couldn't stand anymore, you see, the pain, being unable to walk or do anything she loved. She was such a good dancer when she was young. A county champion was my Maureen. So beautiful too. The illness had robbed her of everything," he paused for reflection, his face twisted with the pain of the memories, "I should have stopped her but she begged me not to. She didn't want me to help as she said I would end up in prison. She didn't want that. She told me to go out and get the paper. I knew she was going to do it and yet, I still left her on her own and when I got back, she…"

Brenda stood shocked and silent. She didn't know what to say. Thank goodness for Winston with his medical training who was coping with the situation calmly.

"It is my fault. I should not have left her on her own. I helped to kill her," again, he broke down in tears.

"Whatever you did, Richard, you did out of love for Maureen," Winston reassured the broken man, "you must never forget that. We can all testify to the fact that you lived for her and did everything for her. I have never known such a devoted couple," he added, "now, Brenda, I need you to stay with Richard while I phone for an ambulance."

At this Richard stood up, barring the door to the front room. "You can't take her away," he shouted, "this is her home. I cannot part from her, she is everything to me. Let me keep her here, we are all right, just the two of us, we don't need anyone else."

Winston gently pulled Richard away and sat him down on the chair again. "Try to get him to drink a cup of tea, Brenda," he instructed as he shut the door of the living room behind him.

Brenda put the kettle on. She felt very much out of her depth. Poor Richard, he didn't deserve this. He had looked after Maureen for so long, never confiding in anyone or asking for help. He was such a proud man. She glanced at him sitting crumpled in the wooden kitchen chair. A shadow of the man she had grown to admire. She made the tea and found some coffee in the cupboard for Winston. She felt this could be a long evening.

"Here you are, Richard, get that down, you," Brenda said gently. She was at a loss to know what to say. Queenie would be good in a situation like this. She would chatter away and take his mind off the situation. Brenda had never been very good at small talk. Even Alan would have coped better, particularly as he was about Richard's age. Did Richard have any family? He had certainly never talked about any. Perhaps they had chosen not to have children because of Maureen's condition? Did he still have siblings alive? Nephews, nieces, cousins? Did he have any close friends?

"Is there anyone you would like me to phone, Richard? Relatives or friends? Someone who could come over and stop with you?"

Richard looked up and put down the tea he hadn't touched. Brenda noticed the tremble in his hands. "We didn't need anyone else; Maureen and I were alright on our own."

"But surely there is someone."

"No," Richard cut her off sharply, "no one."

Winston entered the kitchen shutting the door behind him. "The ambulance will be here in five minutes, Richard. The paramedics will certify the death then we will have to phone the undertakers to take the body. You could hold her hand on the journey there," Winston spoke kindly but Brenda could see the worry in his eyes. How long would Richard survive without Maureen, who he cherished and lived for?

The ambulance arrived and the necessary paperwork was filled in. Winston said he would go with Richard in his car to the undertaker's so he could run him home afterwards, so it would probably be best if Brenda went back to her flat and got some sleep.

Brenda, exhausted, did as Richard suggested, but far from getting any sleep, she spent a sleepless night, thinking about Richard and Maureen. *What an awful way to end your life. What an awful way to end a wonderful relationship.*

Chapter 10

Friday was a blur. She didn't go into the shop as she had already agreed with George that Friday would be her day off. They had sufficient volunteers. Saturday was a busy day, of course, and they were open on a Sunday now, a day Brenda had always felt dragged for her, particularly after her mother died.

The episode last night had brought back memories of when Brenda had called into her mother's on the way home from work, as she often did, to find her still in bed. There was an eerie silence about the place. An indescribable odour. A peace.

Brenda had rung the ambulance, but it was too late. Her mother had died of a severe stroke in the night. They told her that her mother wouldn't have known anything about it. Brenda questioned this assumption, suggested she assumed to make her feel better, less guilty that she had not been there to help her. Still, that was in the past. She must get on with her own life now.

Brenda decided to try and contact Winston. She walked around to his flat and rang the doorbell. There was quite a long pause and Brenda was just about to give up when she heard the cough. Then the front door was opened to reveal Winston in a pair of shorts, looking bleary-eyed and disorientated. On seeing Brenda, he opened the door wider to let her in. She had never seen the inside of his flat before.

"Go through, I will be with you in a minute," he instructed as he disappeared into a room Brenda assumed was his bedroom. Brenda was surprised to see how tidy everything was. She had expected to find a typical bachelor's flat with unwashed coffee cups, magazines and the remains of take-away meals. However, what she found instead was a clean, minimally decorated room, with tasteful art on the walls and books stacked methodically on the table and more books in tightly filled bookcases.

It did not take Winston long to put on a pair of jeans and a brightly coloured, short sleeved shirt.

"Can I make you a cup of coffee, Brenda? I was about to make myself one."

"That would be lovely, as long as it isn't too much trouble. White, no sugar," she added.

Winston disappeared into the kitchen, leaving the door open so Brenda could see a continuation of the organisation and cleanliness she had witnessed in the lounge. He returned with two steaming cups on a tray that displayed a Highland Terrier with a tartan collar.

"Thank you, that is very kind of you," Brenda began. She let her coffee cool in the mug she had carefully placed on a drink's mat that also displayed the same picture of the dog. She wasn't sure how to broach the subject of Richard and Maureen but she was saved the decision by Winston.

"They certified Maureen's death last night. They were very kind to Richard and didn't ask him too many questions, as they could see how upset he was. I knew one of the doctors, so I was able to fill in the missing information. He came home with me. They prescribed a sleeping tablet so, hopefully, he was able to get some sleep last night."

Brenda let that hang in the air for a couple of minutes, then asked, "Did you tell them about the tablets?"

Winston took a long time answering, taking sips of his coffee. He looked tired, nothing like his usual resilient self, "I wasn't asked anything. Apparently, Maureen's doctor was called. They were estimating the time of death. They need to know if an autopsy is necessary. It depends when she was last seen by her doctor."

Brenda took all of this in. Would Richard be accused of assisting his terminally ill wife to die? She knew how much he loved her. She could see that Winston was struggling with the same dilemma as her.

"Perhaps I should pop down and see if there's anything I can get him. I expect shopping is the last thing on his mind," Brenda finished off her coffee that had been far too strong for her and the acidity of it made her feel mildly nauseous. "I'll leave you in peace. You probably want to get some sleep yourself," Brenda added.

Winston snapped back to life, "That's kind of you, I am sure he would appreciate someone to talk to as well. I'm on a late shift so you are right, I should rest or I will be no use to anyone."

Brenda felt he looked far too troubled to sleep but nodded in agreement and returning her mug to the kitchen she said her goodbyes and retraced her steps, then descended to Richard's floor. She stood for a while, wondering what to say. The feeling of sickness had not left her and she wished she had eaten something. That would have helped. She had forgotten all about her Weetabix in the haste of going to Winston's. She would normally never leave the house without juice, cereal, fruit and tea.

She stood for a while outside Richard's door. She wasn't sure what she was going to find if she rang the doorbell. Perhaps she should leave it a few days, perhaps until after the weekend? *No,* she told herself, *nothing like the present*, her mother always used to say.

She could hear the sound of the bell echoing through the hallway of Richard's flat. She rapped on the door as well with her knuckles. Complete silence, and no response. She repeated the ringing of the bell and the knocking on the door with the same result. Perhaps he had gone out? He could have gone shopping or was visiting a relative or a friend. However, Brenda was conscious of the fact that Richard denied having anyone he could turn to and that he and Maureen had lived solitary lives since her illness. A cold panic clutched at her stomach. *What if...?* No, she must not think like that.

Suddenly, the door was open. Richard, unshaven with dark lines under his eyes, the collar of his pyjamas rumpled up, sticking out of a dressing gown that was stained and threadbare. His feet were bare and slightly purplish, his toenails uncut and dirty. This was not the orderly, pristine man Brenda knew. Her heart went out to him.

"I just came down to see if there was anything you wanted from the shops? I need a few things myself so it would be no trouble," she added.

Richard looked bemused, "Things, what things?"

"Well, tea, coffee, milk, bread..."

"Whisky, I could do with a bottle of whisky, wait here," he retreated inside, half-closing the door, returning clutching a twenty-pound note and thrusting it at Brenda, "let me know if it's any more than that, I lose track of prices, rarely go to the shops. Maureen and I used to have our food order delivered on a Monday." With the mention of Maureen, his face crumpled and before Brenda could reply, he had shut the door and silence ensued.

Brenda gathered herself and returned to her flat to get her coat and bag. She checked she had her 'bag for life' and her keys and set off to the supermarket. By now she was feeling quite unwell but fought off the desire to be sick. She still hadn't eaten anything. She would make sure she ate something substantial for lunch. She would treat herself to a take away sandwich. Chicken would be a good choice she felt. Nothing spicy.

The fresh air helped and the supermarket wasn't too crowded. She found the alcohol aisle and selected what she felt was an appropriate brand of whisky. She was no expert, but she had heard of it. She had never tasted whisky herself. Her mother used to like a brandy and lemonade, but Brenda had never taken to it. On special occasions she would have a vodka and cranberry, but she recognised this was probably due to the fact she liked the taste of cranberry juice, rather than the vodka.

Having selected a chicken and salad sandwich on brown, she paid and left the shop, unable to face shopping for any more food. She needed to get back, deliver Richard's whisky and return to her flat for a cup of tea and her sandwich. She might even have a lie down. She was sure she would be fine after a good sleep.

It seemed a long walk back, clutching the shopping. Richard had seen her through his kitchen window approaching the flats, so he was ready at his door to collect his bottle. He refused to take the change and shut the door quickly before Brenda could ask him any questions. Not that she had any intention of doing so as she just wanted to curl up in her own flat, eat some of the sandwich and take a paracetamol.

Chapter 11

The fact that Brenda had promised to go to the auction showrooms on Saturday morning had completely gone out of her head. So, it came as quite a surprise to her when the phone rang at 7:30 a.m. and it was Alan who thought he would just check up on the timings of the morning. *Thank goodness for that*, Brenda thought, *I would never have heard the end of it if he had turned up and I hadn't.*

Pushing the experiences of yesterday to the back of her mind as well as she could, she retrieved the vase that was covered in the bubble wrap it had arrived in and wrapped a hand towel around it as well. *Just in case, better safe than sorry.* She had also written a label to remind herself of its value. Rene Lalique Meandras Vase c. 1935 France. £2,250. She didn't, for a minute, think they would get anything like that. Probably more like a couple of hundred pounds, if they were lucky.

Brenda closed her front door and descended the stairs, past Richard's flat. She felt a wave of nausea pass through her. She didn't know if this was her worry about Richard, or she was coming down with something. She wondered if there had been any further developments. She would try and find out from Winston later.

She walked to the Auction Rooms glad of the fresh air. She didn't feel at all well. Working with Joe Public exposed her to far more coughs, colds and minor ailments. Stomach bugs were notorious for spreading like the plague. *A rather unfortunate simile,* Brenda thought. Her mother had suffered with a weak stomach and lived on Rennies and peppermints. Towards the end she swore there was absolutely nothing that did not give her indigestion.

Alan was already outside waiting anxiously for her. He had wrapped himself up in a thick Barbour that Brenda knew he had grabbed as soon as someone donated it to the shop. It was too big for him but kept him warm. Brenda was feeling quite chilly as she had come out in a bit of a rush and had forgotten her scarf and sheepskin gloves. *Never mind, we would be inside in a moment,* Brenda thought.

"I thought you were never coming," Alan blurted out, "I usually do my food shop on a Saturday morning, so I wouldn't have been pleased if you hadn't arrived."

Brenda nearly retorted that he had asked to come with her not the other way around but left the sentence unsaid, hanging in the air. They both headed into the Auction Rooms and had a browse around the other items. They found an official looking lady with a badge and asked her the procedure for auctioning the vase.

"You ought to have brought it down before the actual day and we could have decided on a reserve price. There is a ten pounds a lot entry fee and we take fifteen percent commission. There is also a charge if you want to have it displayed in our catalogue. Then on preview day, which is the Friday before the actual auction day, the punters come around and look at what's for sale and check an item's condition, make notes on what to bid on, reserve a seat and register for the auction," she delivered this information with weary repetitiveness, "so, you will have to come back next week and we will take a look at your item, I cannot do it now, obviously as the sale is about to begin." With this, she strode off, her badge swinging from side to like the pendulum of a grandfather clock, a few of which were displayed around the room ready to be sold.

Brenda and Alan looked at each other. Brenda still clutching the vase to her chest. Alan looking disappointed at the outcome.

"We could stay anyway. Might be something we fancy. Then go and have a bit of lunch together?" Alan suggested.

Brenda was starting to feel exhausted and distinctly ill. She felt her forehead. Yes, it was hot. She must be running a temperature. However, she felt somehow responsible for how the morning had turned out. How naive of her to think they could just turn up and hope to sell an item on the spot. She could kick herself.

"All right then. I'll just use their toilet facilities first. Go and grab a couple of unreserved seats, I'll be right back." Brenda shouted over her shoulder as she ploughed her way towards a sign stating Toilets. Alan busied himself with the seat allocation task.

Brenda splashed water on her face in the toilets and took her coat off. She was feeling distinctly hot. She knew she should be at home in bed nursing a cup of tea and a couple of paracetamols. She reassured herself that the sale would not take that long, then she could make her excuses and return home. She was also aware of how much Alan was looking forward to his Saturday adventure. She did not think he had a lot going on in his life, hence his regularity as a volunteer at the Charity Shop.

By the time Brenda had returned to the hall, Alan had managed to secure two seats at the back, he was scouring through a catalogue with a frown on his face.

"Bit pricey for me," he complained, "still, it'll be nice to watch the bidding."

Brenda sat beside him. She didn't even have the energy or inclination to look through the catalogue but concentrated instead on deep breathing to combat the nausea. The hall was getting packed and it grew hotter and stuffier. Brenda was aware of hands being held high clutching numbers and the noise of the auctioneers hammer as it was banged on the desk once a sale had been agreed. She vaguely comprehended Alan uttering exclamations if a lot went very cheaply or very expensively. She felt herself drifting off and her head drooping towards her chest. Thoughts of Richard and Maureen entering her brain with frightening clarity. Hospital, police, prison. She felt responsible somehow. She should have tried harder to get in touch with Richard before it was too late. She couldn't bear the thought of him being arrested. Had Winston phoned the police? Would they question Richard? Arrest him? She felt an arm on hers, why were they shaking her?

"Brenda, are you all right?"

Brenda woke sharply, relieved to see the reassuring figure of Alan looking at her with concern. "You were shouting out. Thought I had better wake you. You missed the sale of the Victorian toilet suite with the cracked cistern. Amazing what rubbish people will buy. The set of Golliwogs is up next but who will buy those in this politically correct world? Last time I saw one of them was on the back of a jar of Robertson's marmalade. My sister used to collect the metal badges. She had a line of them on her jacket. There were little figurines as well, I think they were all doing different sports or jobs. Can't remember now. I wonder if she's still got them. Might be worth something now," he ruminated.

Brenda was half-listening. She must get out of here. She was still clutching the vase. "Alan, I'm not feeling too well. I am afraid I will have to return to my flat and go to bed. I wonder if you could find someone who might take the vase to have it registered before the next auction?" She groped in her handbag to retrieve the details of the vase. "If you give this to them, they will know the value of it."

Alan took the vase, "If you wait a moment, I will walk you back to the flat. I don't like to think of you returning alone if you are not well, I could..."

"No, really, Alan, I would prefer to go on my own. I'll be all right once I'm in the fresh air."

With that, Brenda picked up her bag and made her way to the exit, with the sounds of the auction fading as she closed the door behind her, and headed for her route home. She felt very disorientated, almost as if she was in a fog. She was glad she had handed the vase over to Alan as she was sure she would have dropped it. It would take her about twenty minutes to reach her flat. If she took a short cut past the estate, it would be quicker. She normally avoided this route as there were too many teenagers doing wheelies on their bikes and taking their lives in their hands-on skateboards. Still, she just wanted to get back as quickly as she could today. She would feel better once she got back home.

"You all right," Brenda was aware of a young voice, it echoed in her brain that seemed to be in a fog, "You went down wiv a right bang. You've 'it yer 'ead. Don't look too bad, just a lot of blood. You got an 'anky or tissue?"

"In my bag, I think," Brenda replied as she tried to get up from her undignified position on the pavement. She was aware of a wet, snuffling nose pushing at her head. "Go away," she cried, trying to negotiate standing up with trying to find her handbag and pushing the creature's face away from hers at the same time.

"Oh, that's only Max. 'e wouldn't 'urt a fly. Max, leave the lady alone, good boy, sit." The dog obediently sat by his mistress, looking up at her with adoring eyes. "'ere's yer bag, caught one of the kids trying to have it away. He got a slap 'round the ears for it, little tyke. Told him I knew yer, 'e won't try that again."

It was only then that Brenda recognised her saviour. It was the girl who rescued her handbag. How ironical, she thought, that she was doing it again. "Thank you so much. I'm not feeling very well, I just need to get home and rest," she explained, brushing her coat down and attempting to straighten her hair.

"I'll walk back wiv yer. I'm Britney, by the way, and I know you are Brenda. You ain't safe on yer own," she instructed, taking control of the dog and linking Brenda's arm.

Somehow, it was rather comforting having this young girl's arm through hers. Brenda had always had to be independent, particularly after her mother got dementia, then died. She had never had a close friend or a sibling to lean on, so this was a new and welcome experience for her.

Britney chatted all the way back to the flat. She told her she was leaving school after her G.C.S.E's and wanted to work with animals. All her friends were leaving as well. One wanted to be a beautician, another a hairdresser and Sophie wanted to join the Army. Brenda couldn't help but think that would come as a shock to Sophie once she realised the discipline and hard physical training it involved. Perhaps it would be the making of her; handbag thief to army recruit.

Britney tied Max up outside the flats. He sat down obediently and watched his mistress walk Brenda through the doors. She was glad of an arm to hold on to as she walked up the stairs. Everything was starting to look hazy and she felt so weak.

Britney insisted on making Brenda a cup of tea before she left, giving her mobile phone number to her and taking Brenda's number, "In case you need something doing or some shopping. Now, you get to bed, I'll ring yer tomorrow."

It was with a warm glow she put herself to bed, she felt exhausted but strangely comforted by the attention Britney had showed her. There was so much good in the girl. She must pay her back somehow, she thought, drifting off into a deep sleep.

Chapter 12

The sound of her phone ringing woke Brenda up. It took her a while to realise what the noise was and then she felt too weak and tired to move. *They'll ring back if it is important,* she thought. She was settling back into her pillow when a guilty thought struck her. Britney said she would ring her and she had been so good to her yesterday. She glanced at the clock – 1 p.m. She had slept nearly 24 hours. That was unprecedented. She felt her head. It was a bit cooler now. Getting a glass of water, she got to her phone and rang Britney's number. Just as she did so there was a quiet knocking at her door. *Who on earth could that be?* thought Brenda, finding her dressing gown from behind her bedroom door. With the phone in her hand she opened the door a crack to see the worried face of Britney staring back at her.

"I did ring first to say I was coming up but there was no answer, so I thought I'd knock to see how you was."

"I was still in bed, slept like a log. Would you like to come in and have a cup of tea?" Brenda offered.

"Wouldn't mind. Can't stay long. Got to get back to the kids cos me mum's going out later. I tied Max up outside and 'e gets upset like if he can't see me, but 'e'll be okay fer five minutes. I'll make the tea though, you sit down before you fall down," she instructed. "'Ow you feeling?" she shouted from the kitchen.

"A lot better, I don't know what it was, some bug or other I picked up from the shop maybe? I have also been very upset about the death of a neighbour and the effect it has had on her husband."

Before she knew where she was, Brenda was sitting with this teenage girl she hardly knew, telling her the whole story of Maureen and Richard and her dilemma of the ethics of the whole thing. Somehow, she knew it would go no further. After she had concluded her story, there was a long pause as Britney sipped her tea staring out into space, contemplating what she had been told.

"It's simple 'in it. He loved her too much to see her suffer anymore. She couldn't stand her life, what there was left of it, anymore. She asked 'im to help her, so 'e did by letting her store up her pills and getting out of the way whilst she did it," she swallowed the last of the tea, "he just done her a favour. The last thing he could do for her."

Brenda admired this straightforward logic, no ifs or buts, "I worry though, that it is against the law in this country to assist a suicide."

"Law's an ass then," Britney responded, banging her empty cup down on the coffee table, "I'm going to make yer some toast then I had better be off."

With that she took Brenda's kitchen over, finding the bread, butter, a plate, knife and the toaster, "Do yer want a bit of jam on it?"

"That would be lovely, Britney, make yourself some as well."

"Thanks but I'd better be off," she replied, "but I'll take a slice to be eatin' as I walk back."

She completed the task and on settling Brenda in her favourite chair and turning the news on for her, she left, promising she would call her to see how she was tomorrow and not to worry about Richard.

The silence hit Brenda once Britney had left. What a lonely life she led. Thank goodness for the Charity Shop. She would go in again tomorrow if she felt all right in the morning.

Chapter 13

The piercing ring of the phone woke Brenda. She had been dreaming about being in prison, which she assumed was spurred by her worry about Richard. She pulled on her dressing gown and hurried into the sitting room before whoever it was rang off.

"Brenda, it's me, Alan," his voice sounded distant, "I am on my grandson's mobile phone, so I will shout so you can hear me."

"No need to do that, Alan, I can hear you perfectly well."

"I wanted to know how you were, you seemed very poorly on Saturday, I have been worrying about you all weekend, so I thought I would ring you and find out," he gabbled, obviously finding the whole procedure embarrassing.

"I think I'm fit enough to go to the shop this morning. I have had plenty of rest and taken a lot of Paracetamol. Should be there by 10 a.m. at the latest. I am glad you rang, Alan, I have been sleeping like a baby and I could have overslept."

"Well, if you are sure you are all right, I will see you there. I'll have the kettle on," he added.

It didn't take Brenda long to shower, have her Weetabix and don her outfit for the day. It was a relief to be heading towards the shop and though she felt weak, she knew she had got over the worse. *Made of strong stuff, us Watts*, she said to herself.

When she got to the shop, Alan, true to his word, had got the kettle on. George was going to be late again, Mother problems and Queenie was on her way, trouble with her car. So, Alan had opened up and was clearly pleased to see

Brenda, helping her off with her coat and making her sit down to have a cup of tea before starting work.

They had just finished their tea and custard creams when there were the sounds of an altercation from the shop. Brenda got up quickly as there was no one on the shop floor and saw two young men searching through the rack of suits. One was already smartly dressed in a dark-blue, three-piece suit and a contrasting red tie. His shoes shone and he even had a red carnation in his button hole. His companion was, in contrast, dressed in jeans, a T-shirt with the name of some group Brenda had vaguely heard of, and a pair of trainers that had seen better days. He looked a bit worse for wear and in need of a shower.

"Stupid idea of Greg's to lock you in that f...ing cupboard, then hide the f...ing key and leave f...ing clues for us to find you. I didn't even know about it until this morning. You should have left with me and kept a clear head."

"I fell asleep in there. When I rang you, I had been let out by the pub manager. He thought it was hilarious. The wedding's in an hour, my outfit is in Edinburgh and everyone has arrived already that could bring it for me. We will have to find something and quick."

Brenda and Alan had been listening to this going on and didn't know whether to laugh or cry.

"Oh, could you give us a hand here, we are looking for a dark-blue suit as near to mine as possible, a tie and a pair of smart shoes," the suited one explained, "this plonker here has managed to forget to collect his suit from Edinburgh and get very drunk instead and end up being locked in a cupboard. I am his best man so, at least, the ring is safe."

Brenda and Alan sprang to the challenge. After several suggestions, they had sorted the unfortunate groom out with the required outfit, albeit a size too large and the shoes a bit tight. They struggled with the tie but Alan used the Charity Shop link and the Heart Foundation shop had one. The young man put on all the clothes in the changing cubicle and Brenda put his own clothes in a bag. It looked as if he wouldn't be able to have a shower, but at least he looked respectable. His friend handed him a carnation, paid for the goods and used his mobile phone to summon a taxi. They both then rushed off after having thanked Brenda and Alan for their help, almost knocking Queenie over as she was about to open the door to the shop.

"'Ere, watch where yer going," she shouted at their retreating backs.

Brenda and Alan were both laughing so much it took them a while to speak comprehensively. The laughing had brought on one of Alan's coughing fits, so he had to go out to the back room to recover, whilst Brenda related all. Queenie could hardly believe it. "You couldn't make that up if you tried," she said, "wouldn't want to marry a man who forgot to pick up his suit and got locked in a cupboard instead. She should have chosen 'is best man."

After that exciting start to the day, they settled down to the everyday task of sorting through the numerous bags. There were always more on a Monday, Queenie told Brenda, as a lot of people dumped sacks of mostly unusable clothing outside the front door, over the weekend, next to Patrick. Brenda was introduced to the rag bags where clothing that was marked, stained, ripped or so worn it would be worthless, was deposited. The Charity Shop got paid by the bag for it. Not a lot, but every little help.

The rest was sorted into piles to be steamed and that was Brenda's task today. She loved using the steamer, watching the creases disappear as if by magic. She had been working on this for about an hour when she thought she could hear voices in the backyard where people came with their cars to deliver larger goods or pick purchases up. The voices were raised and foreign. Brenda did not recognise the accent. She never had been very good at languages at school and only had a minimal knowledge of French. She relied on that handy phrase, '*Parlez vous anglais*?' The voices were obviously arguing and she thought she heard the sound of ripping material.

"Can you hear that fracas going on out there?" she asked Queenie, who was bent over a very full bag of shoes and handbags.

"What? I can't hear nuffing. Probably kids."

Brenda carried on steaming, but still she could hear the raised voices and obvious disagreements. She put down the steamer and opened the back door. A gush of cold air entered the back room.

"'Ere, what you doing Bren? It's bleeding freezing with the door open," Queenie complained.

"Sorry, I just wanted to put my mind at rest that there was nothing untoward going on outside. Do you mind if I just had a quick look? I know I am a worrier. Mother always said I would worry about not having anything to worry about."

"Go on then, probably best to be safe than sorry," Queenie added.

Brenda pushed the heavy fire door open, enough to slip through without letting too much cold air in. She was certainly not prepared for the sight that met her eyes. There were about ten women of all ages pulling out items of clothing from tall containers that Brenda had not noticed before. Some of the women were holding children by their legs so that they could reach in for the garments and pass them back to their mothers, aunts and grandmothers. Two women were arguing over a dress and were using it as a tug of war, inevitably the article ripped leading to a tirade of language that Brenda assumed was obscene. Their own bags were lined up beside them, some already full to the brim. The determination and vigour of the whole operation amazed Brenda and for a few minutes, she stood watching. She shook herself. They were obviously stealing stock. There was something very immoral about stealing from a charity shop, but the desperation of it affected Brenda. She didn't know whether to be angry or feel sorry for them. She knew she must go and tell Queenie.

She reversed back into the shop and related what she had seen to Queenie, who did not even wait for the full story before she was out of the door, freezing cold or not, heading for the miscreants at full speed.

"What the 'ell are you lot doing nicking our goods. Put that stuff back, it ain't yours to take. If you want anything, then go around the front of the shop and pay for it like everyone else 'as to," Queenie shouted at them.

One of the women approached Queenie menacingly and, in broken English, she shouted back, "These cloths are not yours, they not in the shop. We found them, so ours."

"You've bleeding prised the lid of them containers, they was bolted down, so don't give me none of that," Queenie replied, hands on hips.

All the women started to gather around, shouting things at Queenie in their own language. Brenda started to worry about Queenie. She then had an idea. "We have phoned the police, they will be here very soon," she lied.

"What they do. We only take rubbish out of big bins. They do nothing."

"You need to put those garments back before they arrive," Brenda continued.

The rest of the women and children by now had got the bags full of the merchandise and were moving away out of the yard. Brenda and Queenie were helpless to stop them. There was nothing they could do against so many and they knew they would not think twice about physically threatening them. It was certainly not worth the risk. Having seen that the rest of the group had escaped with the bags, the remaining English-speaking woman followed them, leaving all the mess of their theft behind them. There was nothing else to do but clear up as well as they could. The container lids were broken so they just pushed them against the wall, rescued the few garments not deemed to be worth taking and retreated inside.

"Them containers are where we keep all the good stuff until it comes into season. Some we send to our Premium stores that sell more expensive items. We have lost some good stuff there," Queenie lamented. Brenda had never seen her so down, "it's 'appened before. They pass on information between 'em, so they know where to go. I had better ring the other charity shops and warn 'em." With that she went on to the shop floor to tell Alan and then into the back room.

Brenda felt quite shaken up by it all. The situation had been quite threatening. *The police,* she thought, *I had better ring them,* so she followed Queenie into the back room to tell her what she was doing.

"Nor a lot of point, but do it anyway so there's a record of it, police can't do a lot. They can never find 'em and if they did, it would be proving they had stolen it from 'ere. Each time it 'appens, they come around take the details and we 'ear no more."

Brenda dialled nine 999 and related the problem. She was told they would get a visit from a police officer as soon as was possible. She then put the kettle on.

"Shall I nip out and buy some sandwiches?" she suggested, trying to lighten the situation.

"Good idea," Alan immediately responded, "I'll have ham or chicken." Alan's appetite had obviously not been affected by the events.

The tea Brenda had had earlier was making her desperate to relieve herself, so before she put her coat on to venture into town, she visited the tiny toilet at the rear end of the shop. She smiled to herself, as she always did, at the wooden plaque hanging on the wall above the spare toilet roll.

'Our Aim is To
Keep This
Bathroom Clean.

Gentlemen,
Your Aim Will Help
Stand Closer
It's Shorter Than
You Think.

Ladies,
Please Remain Seated
For the Entire
Performance'.

It was so simple, but inspired. Brenda wished she could come up with such witty expressions. She washed her hands with the orange-smelling liquid soap, then couldn't find the hand towel, so resorted to a tissue she always had tucked up her sleeve.

She shouted out that she wouldn't be long and made her way through the town centre to M&S. She was glad their store had not been included in the recent closures of some branches. It would not be the same High Street without it. More and more shops were closing because of high rentals and the onset of internet shopping. Brenda did not like the idea of selecting clothes, shoes, make up, jewellery etc from a faceless screen. She liked to try things on and ask advice from the shop assistants, if she could find one that was not on her mobile phone or talking to a friend. This brought back thoughts of Britney, her large family, the dog and her helpfulness to Brenda in her hour of need. Young people were not all inconsiderate and self-absorbed. She must try and get in touch with her and perhaps invite her over for some tea.

Brenda purchased the sandwiches and made her way back to the shop. By the time she got back, there were two young policemen talking to Queenie and Alan. They had notebooks out and were jotting down what the two of them were saying. As soon as they saw Brenda, they gestured her over, eagerly.

"'Ere's the lady what can 'elp yer, she were the one what caught 'em at it," Queenie proclaimed, "over 'ere, Bren. Tell 'em what you saw."

Brenda really would have rather gone into the back room and eaten her sandwich than relive the awful experience to the young officers. However, she obliged, feeling quite weary. She hadn't realised how much the morning's events had affected her. She hated confrontation. It always left her feeling slightly nauseous and anxious.

The result was as Queenie had predicted. The officers closed their notebooks and explained what a delicate situation it was and they had to be very careful how they approached the travellers as they could be accused of discrimination. However, they would look into it and let them know if they found any of the articles. They did not hold out much hope of even finding the accused, even with the description Brenda had given them.

Queenie stood with her arms folded. She watched the officers leave the store, served a customer with a pack of cards then instructed Brenda and Alan to take their lunch break while she stayed on the shop floor. At the same time, George came pelting into the shop with his coat undone and his hair decidedly dishevelled.

"I am so sorry," he spluttered, scratching his head and moving nervously from foot to foot, "I have spent the whole morning trying to find Mother. She wandered off in the night. I had the fright of my life when I found her bed empty. All she had on was her winceyette nightie and it was freezing cold last night. I called the police and apparently, she was found knocking at the door of the library at three o'clock in the morning. They said she wanted to change her library book and take out 'Tom's Midnight Garden'. She loves that book. She used to read it to me when I was a child. She could have been…" He trailed off, tears welling in his eyes.

Queenie immediately took over, "Right, come on, George, into the back, I'll put the kettle on and we can 'ave a nice chat over a cuppa. Take-over, you two," she instructed Brenda and Alan as she marched George away.

"Oh, well, sandwiches on the hoof today," quipped Alan, "it's certainly been all go. Can't complain about being bored," he added, unwrapping his ham sandwich and biting into it ravenously. Brenda wondered if he ever ate at home. He always seemed to be hungry. The shop was deserted, so Brenda accompanied Alan by eating her lunch, attempting not to drop crumbs, using the cardboard container as a make-shift plate.

"Poor George, he is certainly having a hard time of it with his mother, I know what it's like being an only child. All the responsibility is on you and you alone," Brenda reflected, "I wonder if there is anything we can do to help him?"

"I don't think so. She has carers through the day up until five o'clock, I understand, but it's at night she's the worst. He is going to have to have to put her in a home. He has to work and he is up most nights with her. It's like having a baby, but one that won't grow up. I have been saying for ages to him to get it sorted but he has always says he can cope. It was a disaster waiting to happen. Now the police are involved though, things might get moving. Social Services will have been informed."

Brenda contemplated this information. She knew how hard it was caring for an elderly mother. At times, she could have screamed with frustration. She would have loved someone to have taken over, but on the other hand she hadn't wanted to put her in a home, even though she had dementia. She appreciated the dilemma George was in.

"The care homes are lovely now, like five-star hotels," Brenda added, "I am sure the Social Services will find her a suitable one, hopefully near enough for George to pop in most days?"

Their conversation was interrupted by a tired-looking young lady asking if they had any spare coat hangers for costumes to be hung in a school play with a large cast. Alan explained they were always short of hangers themselves but he sorted out half a dozen for her and she happily left the shop to continue her search down the High Street in the other charity shops.

"Whilst it's quiet, I'll go and sort out the bags left outside this weekend. Then we can swap over later. Everything marked and damaged or without a label goes into the rag bags to be sent to East London Textiles and everything deemed worth selling is steamed, priced and tagged, using the Universal price guide, adding on £2 if it is brand new. Some items sell better in our premium stores, some in our Lower Core Stores. We're in the middle, a Core store. At least it isn't Thursday. We have all the left-over rubbish from a local boot sale, covered in mud and grass. We normally bin it all. It isn't even good enough for rags," Alan shouted over his shoulder as he disappeared from sight, leaving Brenda to absorb all the information.

Brenda was reminded of the valuable vase. She had completely forgotten about it with everything else that had been happening and her being ill. She had left it with Alan to sort out a reserve price before the preview day which would be on Friday. She wondered how he had got on. Keeping an eye on the few customers in the shop, she put her head around the stock room, "What happened about the vase when I left you on Saturday, Alan?"

Alan did not turn around, but his shoulders visibly dropped. "I've been meaning to tell you about that," he responded, still not turning around, "after you left, I found that lady again who we were talking to at the start of the auction and she said I couldn't leave it there as there was a sale on, but to bring it back during the week. I left it on the table whilst I got myself a cup of tea and a muffin and when I got back, it had gone. I looked everywhere. I asked the lady if she saw anyone take it away but she said she hadn't. Some thieving bugger must have had it away."

Brenda was stunned. She didn't know what to say. She could see Alan was very embarrassed. He couldn't even look her in the eye. Sensing her silence, Alan turned around. He looked lost and old. Brenda hadn't the heart to say anything negative to him. It went without saying how sorry he was.

"Never mind, Alan. Just one of those things. We wouldn't have got its true worth, anyway. It wasn't particularly attractive, which is why it ended up in a charity shop. You had better tell George at some point though, or he might think you have done a private deal and pocketed the money."

Alan blushed and turned around again. Brenda had a horrible thought, then pushed it to the back of her mind. *Surely, Alan would never…? No, absolutely not.* He was far too honourable for that. Then she remembered the beautiful onyx lampstand that Queenie and Alan had denied was with the items brought in by the two warring brothers. What had happened to that? Well, she would not get involved.

She went back into the shop. They were not very busy and Brenda spent the rest of her time on the shop floor tidying around, straightening rails, checking everything was labelled and serving the odd customer. She was really getting the hang of things now and felt quite confident in her new role.

After a while, Alan swapped with her and she went into the stockroom to carry on from where Alan had left off. He had emptied all the bags so she did not have any sorting to do, just steaming and labelling. The conversation with Alan was still playing on her mind. He had looked so sheepish when they changed over.

George and Queenie reappeared and came into the stock room to check on Brenda. George looked less harassed.

"If there is anything I can do to help with your mother, George, please say. I have had experience of my own mother who had dementia. I would be very glad to sit in with her one evening if you need to go out."

George looked extremely pleased, if not somewhat surprised. Maybe no one had offered their services before, "That is very kind of you, Brenda. As it happens, I have a meeting of the Train Spotters Society tonight at the Working Man's Club. It will not go on very long and I won't stay for a drink."

Brenda was a bit taken aback that he had taken her up on the offer so quickly but tried not to show it. "Stay as long as you want, George. I'll take my knitting with me and I can put the television on. What programmes does your mother like?"

"She likes quiz programmes and all the soaps. She normally goes to bed by nine-thirty, but I cannot guarantee she will stay there."

Queenie, meanwhile, was donning her coat, putting the closed sign up and generally shutting shop. Brenda, getting the hint, fetched her coat from the back room and got ready to leave.

"I'll give you my address and telephone number," George said, scrabbling around for a pen and a sheet of paper, "It isn't far from where you live but I would advise you to take your car as it will be dark. Just pull into our drive. Mum's car is in the garage permanently now and I don't drive."

With this, Brenda bade her farewells and set off back to her flat. Her mind was full of everything that happened today, she would have a bath when she got back and relax before her evening ahead. She was slightly regretting her offer now as she felt tired. The illness had taken it out of her and the confrontation in the backyard had not helped, followed by Alan's confession.

She was getting to be a very busy person. *Much better than having nothing to do at all,* she thought. It wasn't until she got back to the flats that she remembered Richard.

Chapter 14

Brenda was a bit nervous about knocking on Richard's door. Her last encounter with him had been the delivery of the whisky on Friday and he had look worse for wear. She felt guilty at not having checked on him before. She must make more of an effort and pop around regularly.

She knocked loudly at the door, bearing in mind his age and hearing, and waited. There was no reply. She knocked again. Perhaps he had taken it upon himself to go for a walk or do a bit of shopping. She remembered he had said he and Maureen had no family or friends. She wondered if he had managed to arrange the funeral. If only she had not been ill at the weekend, she would probably have remembered to check whether or not he wanted any help with all the paperwork etc. She wondered if Winston had been down to help him. Memories of that terrible Thursday night came back to Brenda. She so hoped Richard hadn't...no, she mustn't think like that. She was just about to walk away to try and contact Winston when the door opened and instead of Richard, there stood Winston, amusingly clad in a pink frilly apron and brandishing a broom that had seen better years.

"Hi, Brenda, come in, I was just tidying 'round for Richard and I was about to put the kettle on."

Brenda was once again impressed by the kindness of the man. He had obviously been making sure Richard was alright over the weekend as well as coping with his own demanding role as a nurse, and she was only a volunteer and had omitted to show the same concern. She would have to make amends.

"That would be lovely, I will have a quick cuppa and then help tidy 'round."

"No need, I am nearly finished. You go and talk to Richard. He could do with the company. He has been showing me all the old photos of Maureen." With that, he disappeared into the kitchen, leaving Brenda to make her way into the sitting room where the hunched figure of Richard was immersed in turning the pages of a photograph album. His hair wasn't brushed and the collar of his shirt looked greasy. There were stains on his cardigan and he wasn't wearing anything on his feet. She wondered if he was wearing the same clothes that she had seen him in on Thursday. Her heart went out to him. This is where she could help. A woman's touch.

"Hello, Richard. Do you mind if I come and join you? Winston is kindly putting the kettle on, so I thought we could have a chat."

Richard looked up blankly. His blue eyes were bloodshot, his skin looked grey and his cheeks were sunken. She hardly recognised the spritely efficient man she had known, organising the Residents Meetings, always cheerful, always looking out for others. Recognition dawned on him and his eyes brightened slightly, "Brenda, come and sit with me, I was just looking at our wedding day photographs. We couldn't afford a proper photographer, so a friend stepped in. They are not brilliant but we loved them."

Brenda wondered if he was going to start crying as he got out a very grubby handkerchief, but he blew his nose loudly then tucked it away. She sat with him flicking through the grainy, faded photographs. Most of them were loose, as the supports had fallen off the page taking the photo with it, revealing patches of brighter paper underneath. She remembered her mother showing her pictures of her as a small child. Tiny photos taken with a Brownie camera. They fascinated her. Time frozen, a bygone era. Now photographs were taken on mobile phones, sent straight to friend's email boxes or to Facebook where everyone could comment.

"These are lovely, Richard, Maureen was a very pretty woman and you look so handsome and very happy."

Richard smiled at this and closed the small album, stroking its cover fondly. "I have some wonderful memories and one day we will be together again. She is waiting for me, Brenda, I know that. Perhaps it won't be too long. I know I can't live without her. She was my world."

Brenda was saved the need to give an appropriate reply by Winston arriving with the tea. He had managed to find a teapot and matching cups. Again, Brenda marvelled at his domesticity.

"I couldn't find any biscuits or sugar, but I brought some milk with me," he informed us, placing the tray on the newly polished coffee table, "I hope you are both sweet enough?"

"Winston has been helping me plan the funeral. She wanted to be cremated so we are having a service at St Peter's and then on to Grove Road Crematorium. Winston suggested we just come back here afterwards for a sandwich and a cup of tea as there won't be many of us, we had no…" he trailed off exhausted by the speech and the thought of it all. The overwhelming sadness hitting him again.

"Don't worry about that, I can organise the food and drinks. I can send out the funeral cards as well, once you decide who you would like to be there."

"We led such a quiet life, particularly at the end. We never went anywhere or saw anyone. I had the residents' committee but Maureen was not interested in that sort of thing. Too organised for her. We did a lot when we were younger. Ballroom dancing, singing in a choir, walking, swimming. Seems like a hundred years ago."

Brenda considered this, "Have you a telephone book with numbers of friends from the past? I am sure they would love to come and pay their respects. What about relatives?"

"We had no children and Maureen's brother died quite young of a heart attack; I have no idea what happened to his family. I was an only child. I have a telephone book though; I will get it. I keep it in a drawer in the hall by the phone," Richard rose awkwardly from his chair, his limbs stiff from sitting down too much. He looked frail and gaunt, his trousers hanging loosely from loss of weight. He shuffled into the hallway and the sounds of drawers being opened and papers being shuffled about was followed by Richard returning, clutching a black book, detached pages protruding from its middle.

"Not needed it in a long time. Maureen used to write out all the Christmas cards so I am not sure who she is, was, still in touch with. I was dreading having to do it at Christmas as I will have to inform them of her death," he paused and swallowed, trying hard to stop himself crying again. "Get a grip," he said to himself, "get a grip."

"Let's look through it together," suggested Brenda, "you might recognise some names."

For the next hour, Brenda painstakingly went through every name in the book, making a note of the people Richard remembered. Winston carried on cleaning then took off his apron and announced he had to go as he was on a late shift. Brenda hadn't realised how late it was getting. She saw Winston out, promising him she would let him know the result of the search through the phone book, he said he would inform the other residents once he knew the date of the funeral. Maureen's body was still at the undertaker's. Richard needed to organise the church and the crematorium. He would try and do that tomorrow as he had a day off. With that he sprinted up the stairs, leaving Brenda with Richard who seemed exhausted by everything that had been happening. Brenda felt it was time to stop. She found him a microwavable ready meal in the freezer and an individual trifle in the fridge. She laid a place for him at the table and left, reassuring him she would be popping in and out to see how he was. She then rushed up the stairs, remembering she was due at George's in half an hour.

Chapter 15

Brenda was regretting her offer to George that had resulted in her 'babysitting' his mother. She checked out the address with a local map she had bought for this very purpose, it wasn't far so she thought she would walk rather than have to take the car such a short distance. She knew the area quite well but took a torch with her as it would be dark on her way home. It took her fifteen minutes, not too bad.

The house was a 1930s semi-detached with a front garden that had obviously been looked after in the past, but was now getting out of hand with plants needing cutting back and weeds taking over the borders. There was a milk bottle on the step, so she picked it up and rang the doorbell. There was the sound of footsteps descending the stairs and a shout of, "Mother, Brenda's here." Then the door was opened by George, already wearing his duffle coat and his bobble hat. "Come in, Brenda, this is so good of you. Mother is looking forward to meeting you. She is just watching 'Eastenders', never misses a programme."

He led her into the lounge where a little woman with cotton-wool hair, bright-red slippers and a not too clean tartan dressing gown sat transfixed to the television screen. "This is Brenda, Mum," George shouted, "she has come to keep you company whilst I am at my meeting." He kissed his mother on the top of her head, who seemed oblivious to anything around her and gave Brenda her instructions.

"She has a Horlicks about nine o'clock, then you can take her up to bed. Hers is the one at the front of the house. She has her pills with her drink. I have put them beside her Isle of White mug in the kitchen. She should be as good as gold. Any problems, ring me on my mobile," and with that,

George was out of the door not waiting for any questions that might be fired at him.

Brenda sat on one of the chairs then realised she had not even had chance to take her coat off, so she went into the hall and hung her coat over the stair banister and returned to see George's mum standing at the window with the nets pulled back, "Bob should be home soon, he must be working late."

Brenda assumed this was the name of George's father. "He'll be back as soon as he can, I'm sure," Brenda responded, glad she had experienced these sorts of conversations with her own mother, "why don't you sit down and we can have a chat. George has not told me your name?"

The old lady looked at Brenda as if she had only just realised she was in the room, "Who are you?"

"I am George's friend, Brenda. We work together in the Charity Shop. I have heard lots about you and wanted to meet you."

"Who's George? I don't know no George. Who are you? It ain't no good thinking I've got money cos I ain't, so if that's what you are 'ere for, then you are out of luck."

"I am not here for your money, I just want to have a chat with you and then, when George comes home, I will be off."

"He's drugging me, you know, that man that just left. That's why I'm so addled. He puts pills in my food. He thinks I don't know, but I'm not that stupid. He wants my money, but he ain't getting it. Can you call the police?"

Brenda was faintly amused at the thought of George trying to drug his mother. He was kindness itself and not at all materialistic. She thought it best to change the subject, "What happened on 'Eastenders' this week?"

"You're like the rest of 'em. You don't care. All out for yourselves. They will find me dead in my bed one day. Then they will believe me."

"Would you like your Horlicks now?" Brenda ventured.

The old woman looked at her as if she was mad. "I ain't a child. You can stick your Horlicks where the sun don't

114

shine. You can go now. I don't know why you are 'ere. Where's my Bob?" she got up and went to the window, pulling back the nets, "He ain't usually this late."

Brenda was at a loss what to do. Her own mother had never got nasty, only confused and forgetful. Poor George, he must have been going through agonies trying to work and look after his mother. No wonder he was sorting out a suitable home for her.

Then, from nowhere, came a heart-rending sob, then floods of tears as the old woman crumpled in front of the window, her head and the palms of her hands on the pane of glass. She cried and cried until Brenda steered her back to her chair, trying to calm her down as you would a child, rubbing her back and reassuring her all was okay and Bob would be back soon. Nothing would comfort her. Brenda was in a state of anguish and was just about to ring George on his mobile when a transformation occurred on the old lady. A large, fluffy, black and white cat had quietly entered the room and was rubbing its back against the old lady's legs, meowing pitifully for attention. The crying stopped immediately and she scooped the cat up and sat him on her lap, crooning at the hapless creature and stroking its head. "You love Mummy, don't you, Willie? You wouldn't leave me." The cat purred contentedly and the old woman became calm, rocking in her seat and humming to herself until her eyes closed and she lay back in her seat and went to sleep, exhausted with her emotional outburst.

Brenda sat on the other chair and marvelled at the healing power of animals. She had read about how dogs were taken into hospitals and care homes to cheer the patients and residents up. How they loved to stroke them and talk to them. They were not judgemental, critical or exploitive. They were just loving. Brenda wished she could have a pet but it was against the rules in her flat. Mr Patel had made that very clear. He had a tenant once who had smuggled in a pet white rat and it had escaped and was spotted by Mrs Kershaw who was frightened to death and reported it to Pest Control. This ended up with every flat being inspected for vermin, the rat eventually being trapped and returned to its owner who had owned up, red-faced and Mr Patel, furious at the upheaval, giving him notice to quit. No pets were allowed after that!

After a few minutes, George's mother was asleep with Willie curled up in her lap. She made herself a cup of tea and awaited George's return. She must have nodded off herself because the next thing she knew, the door was being opened and in rushed George, duffle coat undone and bobble hat at a precarious angle. "What happened? I have just got this call from the police to say my mother was found wandering through St Andrew's graveyard holding a cat, which, I assume, is Willie. I'm off to collect her but wondered if you were all right. I blame myself leaving her in the first place, she is such hard work and…"

"I am so sorry, George," Brenda interrupted, "I fell asleep. Your mother was asleep with the cat on her lap, I don't know what to say, she looked so contented. She could have been knocked down, I am so, so sorry." Brenda was almost in tears, feeling George's distress and her own inadequacies.

"No, I should have warned you that she was likely to try and get out of the house if given half the chance," he took off his bobble hat and scratched his head. Brenda noticed he had started to thin on the top. He looked tired and considerably older, "maybe the Social Services will listen to me now. She needs twenty-four-hour care; I can't look after her anymore. One day, she will really hurt herself or set the house on fire."

"Let me go with you to the police station. I can at least help you bring her home. We can pick my car up en route," Brenda was on her feet and collecting her coat as she spoke, eager to be doing something in her embarrassment at letting George down, "come on, it won't take long to get there." With that, Brenda was out of the door, refusing to listen to George's protestations.

They picked up the car and made their way to the Police Station, which, she reflected, was scheduled to be closed in the New Year, adding to the many Council cuts. *Shame*, thought Brenda, *another familiar town feature to be replaced by luxury flats, as if there weren't enough already, and no facilities like schools, doctors or dentists to serve the many new residents.*

When they arrived, they spotted a young female police officer who was holding George's mother's hand, who, in turn, was holding Willie who was squirming about, obviously unhappy with his captivity. They filled in various forms and were told that she had been found in the High Street trying to get into an off-licence, apparently to get Bob his Guinness. George explained that Bob was his father, who died years ago and apologised for wasting their time and said he was going to try and get his mother residential care.

Together they got George's mother and Willie into the car and went the short distance back to the house. George looked worried and tired. Brenda wondered how much sleep he managed to get now. He must be constantly on the alert for his mother's wanderings.

Once his mother was in her bed and Willie had been fed, she put the kettle on and made George and herself a welcome cup of tea. He looked a bit more relaxed and related his battle with Social Services over the care his mother was entitled to. It was as obvious to Brenda as it was to George that the old lady needed to be in a care home but they would have to sell her house to cover the fees. He didn't know where he would live. He had no savings to speak of and would be unable to buy anywhere locally as property was so expensive.

"You live here, George, they won't render you homeless."

"How will I afford to pay Mother's care home fees then if the house is not sold?"

"I will look into it; I am sure this is a common problem. Just try to relax, drink your tea then get an early night. You will feel better in the morning," Brenda was not at all convinced of this but she suddenly felt very tired herself and not too sure how she had got so involved in George's affairs.

Soon after this, she gathered her belongings and made her way back to her flat. It was not long before she was fast asleep.

Chapter 16

She had slept well that night, waking refreshed and ready for another day at the Charity Shop. It was a cold morning and she turned up her central heating and sat in her thick dressing gown, eating her breakfast and reading another few chapters of her Margaret Forster novel. She was lost in the world of the 1800s when there was a light, apologetic tapping on her door. *It must be the postman,* she thought with an overlarge envelope or parcel. Brenda rarely received any mail. Correspondence seemed to be mainly through e-mail or texting nowadays, a system Brenda would never fully appreciate. She still liked to put pen to paper.

"Coming," she shouted, wrapping her dressing gown around her tightly and leaving the safety chain on she peered out of the gap to see who it was.

There stood Britney, shivering in the cold with only a thin leather jacket on and a red and white woollen hat with an outsized bobble on it. Clasped in her hand was the gloved hand of a small child who seemed like a smaller version of Britney, her nose running with the cold and her face streaky with tears. With her free hand she was employed with sucking her thumb through the glove. Her eyes were fixed on Brenda with a steady penetrating gaze.

"I am so sorry to trouble you, but I didn't know what to do wiv 'er," Britney explained, looking down at her miniature self. "Me mum's ill again and I daren't take another day off school. We've got mocks and if I miss 'em, I won't be able to take the real ones. I've even revised for 'em," she added proudly, "I know you ain't got a proper job, like, as you only volunteer, not being rude, like, but I wondered if I could leave her wiv you. I can pick 'er up at four o'clock." This all came out in a rush. The child still had her eyes fixed doggedly on Brenda, not even blinking.

Brenda stood transfixed for a moment, then rising to the occasion, she invited them both in closing the door on the cold air. How could she say no to a girl who had rescued her handbag twice and helped her home after her fall? She looked so young and vulnerable, too young to be in charge of younger siblings when she was really only a child herself. "Sit down and I'll make you some breakfast. Toast or cereal or both? I'll put the kettle on again, I could do with another brew, it is such a cold day."

Britney collapsed into the sofa pulling her sister with her who had now removed her thumb and was cuddling up to her sister. "Bit of toast would be nice. She loves it covered in jam if you've got any. This is Beyoncé, by the way. We call her Bey, though. She's a bit shy, like. Don't say a lot. Spect it's cos she's the youngest. Rest of 'em are lads. They are always taking the piss out of 'er cos she still sucks her thumb and…" she stopped to give Bey a hug.

"Well, it is lovely to meet you, Bey. I am Brenda and I don't say a lot either. Probably because I live on my own, so we should get on just fine. I have some lovely strawberry jam. Would you like a glass of milk?"

"She'll have a cup of milky tea with us, Bren, it's what she's used to. Cheaper than giving six kids milk all the time."

Brenda considered this as she made the tea and toast. As an only child, she had never had to be without basics like milk. No wonder both of them looked so under nourished. She wondered what on earth she was going to do with Bey. She had said she was going into the Charity Shop. How could she take a young child in with her, she would be bored stiff? She had better ring Richard and explain the situation to him. She took the breakfast into the two girls who attacked it with relish, strawberry jam trickling all over Bey's face. She gave Brenda a wide grin. Well, at least they were off to a good start, Brenda thought.

"I have just got to make a phone call to say I won't be in to work at the shop."

"You could take her wiv you, she's as good as gold. Just stick 'er in front of a jigsaw or a colouring book, you won't hear a peep out of 'er."

Brenda considered this suggestion. She did seem well-behaved and she knew there were plenty of toys to entertain her. She would see what George had to say about it. Finding his mobile number, she waited for a response. It rang for a while and Brenda wondered if he was still in bed? Then George's voice came on the line apologising that he could not answer the phone at the moment and could she leave a message. So, Brenda related her dilemma and then tried Alan's number with more success.

"Alan, it's Brenda. I am looking after a young child today for a friend. Do you think it would be okay if I brought her with me this morning? She is no trouble. She will sit in the back room and do jigsaws and any other games we have."

"Don't see why not. Queenie has brought in various grandchildren before now. They're no bother, long as you keep an eye on them."

"Oh, I will do and I can take her out at lunchtime to McDonalds. Her sister will collect her after school. See you later."

Brenda put her phone away. Britney was getting ready to go, gulping back the remains of her tea and taking her empty plate to the kitchen.

"Leave all that," Brenda instructed, "you get off to school and I will see you this afternoon in the shop."

"I'll get to you as soon as I can, I can leave after the last exam," she turned around and gave Bev a hug, "now you be a good girl for Auntie Bren, you 'ear?"

The child nodded, looking up at Brenda with big innocent eyes. Brenda wondered what on earth she had let herself into. Still, too late now and she rather liked being called Auntie.

"I'll let myself out, Bren. Cheers for the toast, went down a treat that did." With that, she disappeared out of the door and Brenda could hear her steps fading as she went down the stairs. Bey ran to the window to see if she could see her sister once she reached the carpark. She banged on the window, but Britney had sprinted off.

Brenda took control, "Right, now I need to get changed, so I will leave you in here for five minutes. Would you like me to put the television on? I'm not sure what is on but I won't be very long."

Be looked at her, wide-eyed. She did not seem at all worried that she had been left with a complete stranger. Brenda wondered how often this had happened before. Still, she was glad the child was not upset. She turned on the television. There was a Breakfast Show on and a celebrity, who Brenda had never heard of, had brought in his dog and they were discussing pet behaviour classes.

"Max!" Bey cried out to the television screen. This was the first word she had uttered since entering the flat. Brenda stopped in her tracks. Max was quite like the celebrity's dog, except Max was probably half that breed and half another.

"No, that isn't, Max, but he looks like him, see if you can find out his name whilst I get changed," Brenda suggested as she made a beeline for her bedroom where she quickly got changed into her 'work clothes', as she now liked to call them. She brushed her hair and applied some lipstick and thought, *that will have to do,* and returned to the living room. She nearly fell over Bey who had obviously been waiting for her outside the bedroom door, thumb firmly wedged in her mouth and her saucer-shaped eyes staring up at Brenda.

"Not Max, Billy," she said through the thumb, obviously pleased she had been able to complete Brenda's task.

"Well done, Bey, good girl," Brenda smiled encouragingly at the tiny figure, "now we must make our way to the Charity Shop. You will like all the toys there."

Brenda found her handbag and phone and as a precaution against the cold weather, she found Bey a woollen scarf and matching hat that fitted any size. The child let her put in on for her and obediently followed Brenda out of the front door.

Chapter 17

The walk to the shop had taken longer than it normally did. Bey had announced after ten minutes she wanted a 'wee wee' and Brenda had to make a diversion to the public toilets near the library where Bey had needed no help to enter a cubicle, relieve herself and wait at the sink for Brenda to run some water to wash her hands with. Brenda was quite impressed, wondering whether this was Britney's training or her mother's; she guessed the former. She had then popped into the small Co-op on route for a fruit drink, a banana and a small wrapped cake to keep Bey going until her lunch. Satisfied she had got everything she needed for the child's morning in the shop, she hurried in an attempt not to be too late.

By the time she got there, Bey trailing behind her, the child had re-established the faithful thumb in her mouth, gloves and all. She looked so tiny amongst the rails, so vulnerable that Brenda experienced a new feeling, never felt before, a maternal sense of needing to protect this small child from the inevitable cruelty of the world. Queenie immediately swooped down on Bey, uttering the usual platitudes of how sweet she was and what beautiful eyes she had. Bey just stared at her and carried on sucking her thumb.

"This is Beyoncé, but everyone calls her Bey. I am looking after her for a friend of mine (Brenda didn't think it was a good idea to explain who her sister was). I couldn't get hold of George, but Alan thought it would be okay to bring her with me. There are so many games and puzzles, plenty to keep her occupied and I will take her out at dinner time," Brenda apologetically explained.

"No problem, it is lovely to have a little 'un around. She reminds me a bit of my Stephie's Natalie, she must be about the same age. Loves 'er thumb as well. Mind you it was a Godsend with my Greg. Only thing that got him off to sleep! He was a right little so and so as a nipper. Nice as pie now though," Queenie smiled to herself, "come on, ducks, let's see if there are any toys you fancy." She bent down to take Bey's hand. The small child looked up at her and smiled, recognising the warmth and kindness there, allowing herself to be led to the area stacked with jigsaws, board games, children's books, soft toys etc. Conspiratorially, the two of them bent down to sort out the 'treasures', Queenie chatting away, Bey, having extracted her thumb at last, eagerly pointing at items she approved of.

Alan arrived out of breath. He would have been on time, but George had phoned to say his mother had got out of the house again in the early morning and had been found wandering up the A12 with just her flimsy nightie, clutching her handbag. She could well have been killed if it hadn't been for an eagle-eyed young man on a motorbike who took her to the nearest hospital, not quite knowing what to do with her now most of the police stations had been shut. Luckily, she had her bus pass and railcard with her so they were able to track down George, who wasn't even aware she was not in her bed.

"He felt right guilty but it wasn't his fault." Alan went on to explain the hospital would not release his mum, telling him he needed to find a secure establishment for her before they would allow her to leave as she was a danger to herself. George had apparently been beside himself with worry but he was going to take a few days compassionate leave to find his mother somewhere to go. "He knows he can't cope with her at home anymore. Linda had phoned him to say she wasn't coming in. She has to go to the vets to have her cat put down. So, we are on our own for probably the rest of the week, all hands to the deck," he concluded, almost triumphantly.

Brenda decided not to relate the details of last night's escapade to Alan and Queenie. She would fill them in later.

Queenie had set up Bey with a wooden jigsaw puzzle, sitting her in a small plastic chair and desk that they had not been able to sell and was labelled to be sent to another store. She had got her a small plastic beaker of orange squash she kept in the cupboard for her grandchildren or any deserving cause. She now positioned herself behind the till, defying anyone to attempt to usurp her, so Brenda turned to tidying the racks and Alan went into the store-room, mumbling something about 'sodding steaming again'.

Brenda felt she ought to do something useful and show Queenie she was grateful for her help with Bey, "I'll put the kettle on and get everyone a cup of tea,"

By the time Brenda returned with the tray of tea and biscuits, there was a young woman frantically searching through the size ten skirt rail.

"She's trying to find a plain black skirt and a plain white blouse, Bren, can you 'elp her? She ain't got long. Got to be in work in fifteen minutes."

"I need 'em quick like. I washed me other skirt and blouse with a load of other stuff and the dye ran and the skirt was dry clean only. I 'ave just got a job at Wildwood as a waitress and it ain't going to look too good if I admit I have ruined the uniform in the first week."

Brenda recognised the voice and realised it was Sophie, one of the 'Horrible Teenagers' that had stolen her bag. She wondered if she had realised she was the victim of her crime. She sorted out a couple of size ten white shirts and hung them in the changing area not wanting to get too near Sophie in case she recognised her. She was not in the mood for a confrontation. Sophie ran in with her selected items and could be heard swearing that the skirts were too long and the shirts were too tight. She reappeared having hitched the skirt up by folding it over at the waist and the shirt was open as far as could be just about decent, revealing a hint of a lacy black bra.

"I'll 'ave these," she informed her, "can you put my clothes in a bag for me, I can leave 'em in our staff room."

All sorts of questions were running through Brenda's mind. Why was the girl not at school still? Why had she come back into a shop she had sworn not to return to? Had Britney told her about their acquaintance?

At that moment, she was aware of Bey at her side. She was staring up at Sophie with her big eyes. The thumb had returned to her mouth and she pushed her other little hand into Brenda's.

Sophie caught sight of her, "What you doing 'ere Bey? Is Brit wiv yer?"

"I am looking after Bey for her today, Sophie. She is sitting some examinations and her mother is ill again. She will collect her this afternoon," Brenda realised almost immediately that she had called her Sophie, wanting to kick herself for the slip.

"You're that silly cow who 'ad a go at me about the 'and bags aint yer?"

Queenie, realising there was an issue, stepped in, "You finished in 'ere, young lady? That will be £7 for the skirt and blouse and 'ere's the bag you wanted so that is £7.05." She stood with her hands on her hips, daring Sophie to carry on with the insults.

Sophie clicked her tongue and fumbled in her bag for the money, which she presented to Queenie reluctantly, "Only reason I come in 'ere is it's nearest to Wildwoods. Wouldn't be seen dead in 'ere otherwise. There are always geriatrics like you serving, drawing yer pensions, being a bleeding burden on the welfare system." With that, she sniffed loudly and pushed her way through the doors, leaving a stunned Brenda and indignant Queenie, who was surprisingly stuck for words.

Queenie finished her tea in silence, "She's right, ain't she, Bren? We are a burden. The older we get the more we will have to rely on our families. Beg yer pardon, Bren, I know you don't 'ave none. Probably better in a way. Mine will feel obliged to look after me. Told 'em I will go into a home when the time comes, but they won't 'ave it. Watched too many documentaries on failing care homes and abuse by the staff and all that. I shall stay independent as long as I can." Some of the defiance had returned to Queenie and she took her mug into the back room, calling on Alan to do the same if he had finished. The moment had gone. Brenda had witnessed another side of Queenie she had not seen before and as with Richard, it quite disturbed her. People were very complex. Under that outer layer were so many other layers that were not exposed or made obvious to people around them.

Bey squeezed Brenda's hand, "Bey go ting?"

Brenda couldn't work out what 'ting' was. Did she mean the toilet? "Come on then, Bey, it's out the back."

"No, ting!" The little girl pointed at the till. Brenda realised she was referring to the *ting* the till makes as it's opened and shut. "Bey want to ting," she pulled Brenda with her to the counter. Oh, well, it couldn't hurt to give the child a go on the till, she had after all been very well-behaved all morning. Brenda felt bad about her witnessing Sophie's language, although she probably wasn't a stranger to such talk.

"All right then, but you must be very careful. It shoots out very fast. I will get you a chair to stand on." She retrieved the chair Queenie had found for Bey to sit on and got her to stand up with Brenda holding on to her under her armpits for stability. She showed her how to release the till so it shot out.

The child was delighted, letting Brenda show her a few times before she chorused, "Me, me do it!"

Brenda checked there were no customers needing serving. It was relatively quiet and Alan was still in the stock room and Queenie was in the staff room. Bey enthusiastically banged on the keys she had been shown, leaning forwards with Brenda holding on to her. The drawer shot out, hitting Bey firmly in the chest, who pushed it away with a yelp of pain. The till shot off the counter, landing with a sickening crash in front of the blue garments rack, narrowly missing a potential customer, then sliding under the rails with Brenda and Bey looking horrified, unable for a moment to move from their positions.

Queenie, on hearing the crash, rushed out of the back room literally at the same time as Alan sped out of the stock room. They both looked at Brenda who was still holding on to Bey then at the gap where the till should have been.

"What's 'appened to the till?" Queenie asked, unable to see the item in question under the rails.

Brenda took Bey off the chair and, red-faced, rescued the till from its position under the rail, "I am so sorry, Queenie, I shouldn't have let her have a go on the till. She was so keen though and she has been so good this morning. I will pay for the damage."

Queenie inspected the counter where the till usually stood. "The rubber mat aint there that stops it slipping. It aint the little un's fault," she paused, summing the situation up, "why don't you take Bey to McDonalds and we'll see if we can ger it working again?"

Alan had been fiddling about with leads and tutting perceptibly, shaking his head and sniffing with obvious annoyance at the situation. Brenda felt guilty and rued her decision to bring Bey to work with her. Bey was looking anything but sorry, in fact, she looked quite elated. "Ting, ting," she said animatedly, annoying Alan even more.

"No, we are going to see Ronald McDonald and have a nice lunch," Brenda hoped the lure of fast food would be distraction enough for Bey to forget about the till. She was wrong. Having not had a lot to do with young children, she was not used to tantrums. She had heard something in the past about the 'Terrible Twos' but that was as far as it went. To her chagrin, Bey climbed on the little chair again and slammed her hands down on the keys of the till Alan had just repositioned. He attempted to intervene only to be rewarded with the till drawer striking him on his elbow. He uttered various expletives as he rubbed his funny bone walking up and down in obvious agony. Queenie took over, removing Bey from her perch and planting her firmly to the side of her, holding on to her hand tightly.

"Are you all right, Alan?" Benda asked unnecessarily as he so obviously wasn't.

Queenie butted in before Alan could reply. She had suddenly realised there was a customer who had taken herself off to the changing booth without having the items counted. You were only supposed to take in three pieces of clothing.

"Alan, can you sort out that customer?" she nodded towards the booth, "see if she's buying them clothes when she comes out." As if on cue, the curtains were pulled open and a young woman wrapped in a thick purple coat emerged and headed towards the door with obvious speed.

"Nothing suit you?" Alan enquired to her retreating back.

"Obviously not. So rude these youngsters. People had manners in my day."

He went into the booth to collect the garments. He reappeared immediately. "Nothing there!" he exclaimed, "the little thief has had it away with the clothes under that big coat of hers. We need to ring the other shops and warn them there is a thief about." He trundled off into the back room, the till incident forgotten for the moment.

Brenda took the opportunity to get her own and Bey's coat. She sought out her handbag and relieving Queenie of the little girl, she whipped her out of the shop at speed and down the High Street to McDonalds. Bey, taken by surprise, trotted by her side and besides a few more 'ting, tings' seemed to be happy once they reached the restaurant. Brenda wondered what to order. She didn't think Bey would be too fussy, coming from a big family. It was probably a fight for survival with Bey being at the bottom of the pecking order as she was the youngest.

They queued up together and ordered and collected their food. Brenda had not eaten in a McDonalds before, so stuck to fries and a coffee. She could not call them chips as these thin offerings did not resemble the chunkier version she knew from Fish and Chip shops of her youth. However, she found to her surprise she actually enjoyed them. Bey was fascinated by it all and chomped on her fries contentedly. Brenda had got her a milk shake with a straw in it that she soon found made a wonderfully loud noise as she sucked through it and better still if she blew through it made the shake bubble up and spill over the container. Soon there was a river of chocolate shake running across the table on to the floor. Brenda stood up quickly to avoid the stream covering her skirt, removed the shake from Bey and looked around for assistance. No member of staff seemed to be about except from behind the food counter and they were all busy serving an ever-increasing queue. Bey, upset her entertainment had been removed from her, set up a wail that resulted in heads turning and a few disapproving comments about grannies not being able to control their grandchildren. Brenda had not thought about how their relationship would appear to Joe Public. It was quite pleasant to be thought of as a gran. Just as she was about to approach the counter for help or even just some kitchen roll, she heard a *ping* from her mobile she had kept on in case of messages from the shop or even from Winston or Richard. She clicked on messages.

"Finished my exams. Will pick Bey up at the shop soon as I can, Britney."

"That was Britney," she explained to Bey, "we had better get back." She attempted to soak up some of the shake with a few tissues she had in her pocket, then, without meeting the eyes of the people at the adjacent tables, steered Bey out of McDonalds, leaving the milkshake and its spilled contents on the table.

She marched her little companion back to the shop, entering at the same time as George, who held the door open to them. He looked harassed and tired as if he had not slept for a week. That was probably the truth, Brenda thought.

"How is your mother, George?"

"I have managed to have her assessed and Social Services are looking into finding her a place in a care home. She owns the house though, so I think I will have to sell it to afford the fees. I don't know what I'm going to do, I just assumed I would stay on in the family home after my mum had…"

Brenda knew that couldn't be right. George could not be left homeless. "No one will chuck you out onto the streets, George, it is your home. Let's go through the back. This is Bey, by the way, I am looking after her for a friend, but she is being collected in a minute."

Queenie had gone home. "Back playing her up," Alan informed them, "and Linda had phoned to say she wouldn't be in as she was waiting for a plumber to mend her toilet, but I could stay on."

George, Brenda and Bey went into the back, leaving the door open so Brenda could see when Britney arrived. George was slumped in a chair, his hand covering his eyes. "What am I going to do, Brenda? It is all such a mess. I don't want to put her in a home, but I can't manage her anymore. Such a mess."

Bey let go of Brenda's hand and went over to the reclining figure. She stroked George's head gently, making hushing noises, her little face looking troubled at the obvious distress George was showing. Brenda was amazed at this response from one so young and George opened his eyes and was obviously touched by this display of concern. Just then, the sound of Britney arriving in the shop and asking Alan where Bey was brought them back to the present and Brenda gently took Bey's hand again and led her into the shop, where Britney was waiting for her sister.

"Hi, Bey. You been a good girl for Auntie Brenda?"

Bey had inserted the thumb again so she just nodded, cuddling up to her sister's legs, looking up to her with wide eyes.

"She has been an absolute treasure," Brenda reassured her, "we have had a wonderful time. How were the exams?"

"All right. Didn't do too bad, I suppose. Got 'em all week. Me mum's okay though, now. Thanks for today, though," she gathered Bey up who was jumping from foot to foot in her eagerness to get away, "you done well though.

She can be a little madam when she wants." Brenda thought it best not to mention the till or the milk shake.

Chapter 18

The rest of the day had passed quietly and Brenda had slept well that night. She hadn't realised how exhausting looking after a young child could be. So, when she woke up on Wednesday morning she felt refreshed and ready to tackle another day. She made a mental list of things to do.

Call in on Richard on the way to work.

Call in on Winston on the way back from work.

Suggest to George to ring Citizens Advice Bureau about financing his mother in a care home.

See what was on at the cinema.

The last item was spontaneous. Since her life had so changed, she thought she would start going out more and if that meant going somewhere on her own, then so be it. She toyed with the idea of asking Richard but then thought that was too soon after Maureen's death. She didn't even know when the funeral was yet. She would ask him later.

After a leisurely breakfast, she gathered her belongings for the day and made her way down the stairs to Richard's flat. She rang the doorbell. She could hear the sound of a radio playing and a slightly out of tune voice accompanying the song. *That is promising,* Brenda thought, *he must be feeling a bit better.* She rang the bell again. She knew Richard's hearing was not too good and he had a hearing aid which he rarely remembered to wear, preferring instead to ask people to speak up. The singing stopped and there was the sound of shuffling feet approaching the door.

"Who is it?"

"It's Brenda, Richard. I've just stopped by to see if there is anything you want from the shops or anything I can help you with generally?"

The door opened and Richard, still in his dressing gown, indicated for Brenda to step inside. "Don't want the world and my wife seeing me in my stripy flannelettes. That's what I miss about going to work. A purpose to get up and get dressed."

Brenda knew exactly what he meant. She had felt like that before she started volunteering at the shop. She remembered the long days she filled half-heartedly with trips to the shops, the library, the endless coffees in the High Street cafes. Glad of any diversion, a welcome chat or smile from a stranger. A dog rushing up to be stroked, a visitor to the town asking for directions. Anything to stave off the boredom of retired life on her own. Yet she should really count her blessings. She owned a flat, had a decent work pension and her state pension had started at sixty unlike the women who had to wait until they were eligible by dictate of when they were born. One of the Residents' Group had to wait until she was sixty-seven.

"You look a bit better today, Richard. I am on my way to the Charity Shop so I cannot be too long, but if you want to write me a list, I can shop for it on my way home tonight." Then Brenda had an idea that she didn't think Richard would take up. "Would you like to come back for your tea tonight? It will only be something simple, an omelette or some salmon. We could have a good chat." Then fearing this invitation may look a bit forward, she added, "I can ask Winston as well, he works so hard I bet he never has time to eat properly."

There was a pause and Brenda wondered if she had gone too far, so soon after Maureen's death, she should have waited until after the funeral. That reminded her. Richard had not informed her of the date of the funeral or where it was going to be. She had no idea if Maureen and Richard were religious. She was not aware of Richard talking about going to church or seen them leaving regularly on a Sunday to attend.

"That would be very nice," Richard's reply took Brenda by surprise, "what time would you like me to arrive?"

"Seven o'clock would be fine. I will pop into the shops on my way home and I should be back at the flat by five thirty. That gives me enough time to tidy 'round and cook. I will phone Winston from work on my mobile."

Richard nodded, steering Brenda out of the front door and standing with her in the corridor, "See you then," he responded, retreating into his flat, spurred by a tenant walking past eyeing his pyjamas and stubbly chin quizzically

Brenda stood for a moment, surprised at both her forwardness and Richard's reply. She then smiled to herself and continued on her route to the Charity Shop, having forgotten her original reason for calling on Richard, to see if there was anything he needed. Or had he told her that in his reply to her suggestion of tea with her...and Winston, of course.

By the time she reached the shop, Brenda had planned the meal.

Chapter 19

Queenie was up a stepladder with Alan holding on to the sides of it firmly, giving instructions as Queenie attempted to pin up a Christmas garland displaying the message *Happy Christmas*. George was behind the till, showing a youth how it worked. The lack of interest was obvious as the young boy kept glancing at his phone and shuffling from foot to foot with intermittent sniffs.

"Morning, or should I say, afternoon?" Alan commented.

"You're here now, no problem. Can yer put the kettle on Bren? I think Alan needs a custard cream. He's been bad tempered since he came in."

"Sorry, I'm late, I was checking on an elderly neighbour and the time just went. I had forgotten it was so close to Christmas. I will give you a hand after I've made the tea. I have a good head for heights. Mother suffered from vertigo, so I was always the one to reach things from high cupboards or go up the loft to retrieve the suitcases or the Christmas decorations we stored up there."

"Custards, Bren," Queenie reminded her.

While Brenda was putting the mugs out and filling the kettle, George flustered in with the youth tagging on behind him. He acknowledged Brenda and introduced the youth whose name was Wayne. He was here for the Christmas period on work experience. "Couldn't get a job nowhere else," he chimed in. George then proceeded with the same induction that Brenda had experienced, hurrying through it, anxious to rid himself of the responsibility of this disinterested pupil. Brenda had just lined all the mugs up on a tray when she realised she should probably offer Wayne a drink.

"Wayne, would you like a tea or a coffee?"

"You gor any Coke? Don't do tea or coffee. It's naff."

Brenda looked at George for the answer, then realised how futile that was as George would have no idea what the contents of the cupboards would reveal, so she went into the shop to ask Queenie who was still struggling with the banner. Just at that moment the door was pushed open by an elderly gentleman and a large Rottweiler bounded past him into the shop. The over-zealous creature did a circuit of the shop, knocking a variety of clothes off their hangers and inducing cries of alarm from potential customers who rapidly vacated the premises. Queenie wobbled on her ladder dropping the banner which found its way unfortunately across the dog's eyes blinding it momentarily but enough to induce panic as it shook its head rigorously and careered into the ladder and the terrified Queenie, who was hanging on for dear life, with Alan failing miserably to steady her. Brenda dropped her tray with the shock of it all, adding a stream of hot liquid and custard creams to the mayhem. The dog then slipped in this and skidded down the length of the shop, landing unceremoniously in a pile of jigsaws that Alan had meant to stack on the shelves but had forgotten.

The old gentleman, meanwhile, was still at the door, calling the dog's name, Tyson, repeatedly but ineffectually. He had a lead in his hand and once the dog had landed, he started to make his way down to the heap of dog and jigsaw.

"You are a naughty boy," he admonished the dog, "this is not like you at all." The response was a loud, menacing bark from the dog and a cry of alarm from Queenie who was still on her perch with Alan holding on to the ladder tightly.

George and Wayne had appeared from the back room and were both gaping at the chaos the dog had caused.

"Ought to be muzzled, that dog. My uncle's got a Rottweiler. Never lets it off a lead after it bit a jogger in the park. She were going to ring the police if she saw 'im wiv it again without a muzzle on. They put 'em down you know if they get complaints in to say they are biting people," Wayne said all this, keeping a decent distant between him and the offending animal.

George now attempted to take charge, feeling it was his place as manager. He had never been a dog lover and, in fact, had harboured a fear of them from his childhood.

"Could you secure your dog on a lead? I will have to take down some details about the incident and…" He got no further than this before Tyson, realising that his master was in trouble, did what any dog worth its salt would try and do, attack the enemy. So, he bounded up to George and embedded his teeth into his hand. This resulted in an agonising cry of pain from George, another scream from Queenie and shocked silence from Brenda and Alan, who, unlike him, had kept out of it up to now.

The owner attempted to persuade Tyson to let go, tempting him with a biscuit he had in his pocket, but Tyson had tasted blood and was not going to listen to anybody until he had conquered the enemy.

"Poke 'im in the eye wiv yer fingers," Wayne instructed, "the dog will soon let go. My uncle did it all the time wiv 'is dog. It worked a treat."

Alan now decided to join in the chaos. "I will ring the police, the R.S.P.C.A. the," he couldn't think who else he could ask for assistance so he took out his phone and started to jab numbers into it as George continued to cry in pain and Queenie scream.

Brenda was completely out of her depth. She had no idea what to do. She had never owned a dog and had never wanted to. The residents in her flat had no pets as it wasn't allowed by Mr Patel on grounds of Health and Safety. As if on cue, the door to the shop was pushed open and there stood Britney with Bey holding her hand and Max on a short lead. Max started to bark as he spotted Tyson, who recognising a fellow dog let go of the now desperate George to run over to sniff at Max. The owner took the opportunity of attaching Tyson's lead and dragging him over to the door of the storeroom where he spoke to the excited dog in tones suitable for an infant, not a dangerous Rottweiler. Brenda couldn't help but think that was probably why the dog took no notice of him. Tyson obviously needed a firmer hand. Meanwhile, she turned her attention to George who was being comforted by Queenie who, seeing the dog was secured on a lead, had descended the ladder and was examining the bitten hand with Wayne peering over her shoulder.

"You need to go to A&E wiv that, it looks right nasty. You will 'ave to 'ave a Tetanus jab," Wayne advised, "my sister got bit once by a Yorkshire Terrier and didn't do nothing about it and 'ad to 'ave a finger off. Not that I want to worry you like."

"Right, that's settled it. We're going to the 'ospital, and sharpish if what Wayne's told us is true," so, ignoring George's protests, Queenie got their coats.

Alan, had been trying to get connected to the 111 number with no luck.

"Ring a cab, Alan, he just needs to be seen by a doctor in A&E, it will be quicker in the long run. Wayne, ger a chair and the first aid box from the cupboard above the sink. We can at least pur a bandage 'round it to stop the bleeding and George can sit down. We don't want him fainting on us."

"Cab will be five minutes," Alan announced, glad he had been of some use.

It was obvious that George was in a lot of pain and Brenda, was feeling rather useless. "Would you like a Paracetamol, George?" she offered.

Alan jumped in here, "He can't have any medication until he has seen a doctor. It might clash with whatever he is prescribed, sorry old man."

"Bleeding dog lovers. Ought to be a law against 'em," Queenie shouted, loudly enough for the dog's owner to hear as she attempted to wrap up George's hand in an insufficient piece of bandage, securing it with a safety pin. The dog owner was still trying to calm Tyson down, but the process was not helped by an excited Max, who was refusing the listen to Britney's commands of 'sit'. Bey, was clinging to her sister's legs with her thumb firmly inserted in her mouth.

"Bey, come with me and I will get you a glass of orange squash," Brenda offered, feeling at least she could be the child minder during the chaos, "we could read a book together."

Reluctantly, Bey detached herself from Britney's leg and put her hand up for Brenda to hold. Brenda, feeling strangely honoured, took the young child into the back room, found the little chair Queenie had used during Bey's previous visit and a colourful picture book. She made the orange juice, putting on the kettle as an afterthought and settled down to reading the book to Bey. When the kettle had boiled, she got up and made tea for everyone, aware that the flood made by the first batch had not been cleaned up. *Oh, well, more important things to think about at the moment,* she thought. She then put a teaspoon of sugar in one of the mugs as she had read somewhere that sugar was good for shock.

Brenda took the tray out. "Here you are, everyone. George, make sure you drink yours," she was aware that George was trembling, slightly so she helped him hold the mug to his lips.

"Taxi for Alan Taylor," a man in a long-sleeved shirt called from the door. Brenda realised she had never got to know Alan's surname. There was so much still to learn about her co-voluntary workers. Queenie gathered George up and they both disappeared up the road in the taxi.

The dogs had calmed down. Brenda assumed that was probably Britney's skill with dealing with dogs rather than the owner of Tyson. She heard some muted conversation about telephone numbers, muzzles and keeping potentially dangerous dogs on a lead and then the door opening and the bowed figure of Tyson's owner crossed the shop floor and without eye contact with anyone, disappeared up the street.

"Think we could all do with that cup of tea and a custard," Alan's voice rang out, much louder than necessary, owing to his poor hearing, "been quite a morning. You sort the little 'un out Britney, I'll tidy up out here with Wayne after my break," Alan instructed, taking on the role of manager with George and Queenie off the scene.

Britney entered the shop with a subdued Max on a very short lead, "Some people shouldn't 'ave dogs, specially dogs like that. He should have a poodle or summut. Could 'av killed someone." She looked genuinely concerned. "Could 'ave been a child. Might be next time. I'm going to check he has muzzled 'im or I'm off to the police. I've taken his name, address and telephone number. He ain't going to get away with it. Is Bey all right? Good thing she's used to dogs, aint it?"

"She has been ever so good, Britney. No problem at all. What did you both come in for?"

"I wondered if you could look after Bey again for us, Bren? I know it's a cheek, like, but I trust you and she likes you."

"When would you like me to look after her?"

"From about 7 p.m. tonight? Me mum's ill again and the boys are all at football training. David says he can pick 'er up at 9 p.m. after his session. I want to go to an Open Evening at the college but my slot is one of the last cos I booked it late, like. I wouldn't ask you Bren, but I really want to go to college rather than get any job that don't need no proper qualifications. Say if you can't do it. I will 'ave to take 'er wiv me. She gets so bored though and I…"

"That is fine, Britney. Bring her 'round at 7 p.m. We will have a lovely time together."

Brenda and Britney went into the back room. Bey was still occupied with looking through the book Brenda had found her. Max had settled down beside her, resting his head on her lap. *What a lovely sight*, Brenda thought.

"Bren, you are a star. I will take her back now and see yer at seven," she organised Bey and pulled an exhausted Max up from the floor. The three of them left the shop as quickly as they appeared.

Brenda put away the little chair and the book. She remembered Wayne's drink and had a futile look in the cupboard. This only revealed more tea bags, a bag of sugar, sweeteners, the custard creams and a packet of out of date

Eccles Cakes. She made Alan's tea again and took this in to him with the biscuits.

"Can't find any squash, Wayne, but I can get some in my dinner hour as I have to buy a few things for a meal I am cooking for a neighbour tonight," Brenda stopped in her tracks. She remembered too late she had promised to cook for Richard tonight and now she had promised to babysit Bey, and at exactly the same time. She must have gone pale because Alan came over to her.

"You all right, Bren? You have gone very white."

"Oh, it's probably the shock of the dogs and George getting bitten. I will be okay in a minute. Do you mind if I have my lunch break now, Alan? I will only be half an hour. Just need to go to Sainsbury's. I will bring my sandwich back with me. Do you or Wayne want anything?"

"Egg and cress," Alan replied.

"Coronation chicken and a packet of crisps," Wayne quickly added.

"Right, well, I'll be on my way. Could do with a bit of fresh air," Brenda replied putting her arms through her coat sleeves.

She was soon on her way. What should she do about tonight? At least she had not phoned Winston. However, the arrangement with Richard had come first and Brenda would honour it. She would just have to ring Britney, she would understand. She fished for her phone in her bag and tapped on Britney's name. A voice replied immediately that the number was not available. *Blow*, thought Brenda, *she's got her phone off. That's all I need.*

She completed her tasks and returned to the shop. The afternoon went by as a bit of a blur as she tried to come up with a solution to the problem. There were two options as she could not contact Britney. Either she cancelled Richard, or Bey could sit watching the T.V. whilst she and Richard carried on with the meal. Neither option was satisfactory.

Chapter 20

By the time Brenda reached her flat, unpacked her shopping and put the kettle on, she had made up her mind. She did not have the heart to cancel Richard and Bey was a lovely little girl who Brenda was sure would behave herself until her brother collected her.

She busied herself with preparing the fish and the vegetables. She had bought a lemon and meringue pie for dessert as she would certainly not have time to make one. She wondered whether to start with soup as she had plenty of cans in the cupboard and the more courses the longer you could take over the meal, chatting between eating the food and then finally sitting in the armchairs for coffee. By then Bey would have gone, so they could talk more freely. It was a long time since Brenda had cooked a dinner for a man; well, for anyone beside her mother and she didn't eat a lot and never liked what Brenda prepared for her. She had resorted to Ready Meals in the end, so when her mother complained, at least it was not a slur against her. She felt quite enthusiastic about the evening and went to wash her face, put a bit of make up on and chose a *comfortable* pair of black trousers and a stripy blouse she had always liked. Her hair would have to do. She did not want to have to wash it and there was a lot you could do with a bit of backcombing and a can of hairspray. She added the final touch of a squirt of perfume she had received as a gift from a girl at work she had given lifts to.

Once ready and the dinner in the oven, the vegetables ready to be turned on, the soup in the pan and the plates on top of the oven to warm them, she laid the table for two, adding a candle as an afterthought. She was quite pleased with the result. She then sat in a chair and turned on the news and waited for both Bey and Richard to arrive.

There was a knock at the door. Brenda checked her watch. Only 6:30 p.m. Perhaps Britney had decided to come early for a chat or Richard had got the time wrong. She opened the door to find Winston looking tired and worried, "Thought you would like to know. Richard had a fall this afternoon. He tripped and banged his head on the concrete in the carpark. He has a nasty bump and suspected concussion. They have taken him to St Luke's. Luckily, I was on duty so that is how I know."

Brenda felt oddly guilty that she had not invited Winston to the dinner, which was the original plan before Bey came into the equation. She wondered if Richard assumed Winston was coming and had said as much to him?

"Come in, Winston, thank you for letting me know. Is there anything I can do? I am a bit stuck this evening as I said I would look after a little girl for a friend of mine whilst she attends an open evening, but I could go tomorrow."

"I don't know how long they will keep him in. They are running a few tests on him, heart, brain scan etc. so they might take a while. Then the doctor has to look at them all and see if he is fit enough to return to an empty house," Winston paused, "I am more worried about the fact that he didn't seem to care what happened to him. He said he just wanted to be left alone and could I tell them to stop poking and prodding him as there must be younger and more deserving patients to see."

Brenda thought about this concerning statement. Richard had seemed okay this morning but a lot of hours had passed since then. Did he feel he was betraying Maureen by accepting a dinner invitation and this had made him feel guilty and depressed? She brushed the thought aside at the same time as hearing a voice on the stairs and then little feet running up them.

There was a loud knocking on the door and Brenda opened it to see Bey red in the face from her run, clutching a blanket to her chest with a writhing, Dutch Rabbit wrapped in it, its ears poking out of its cover and its nose twitching at indecent speed. Britney was not far behind, carrying a packed 'bag for life', its handles straining with the weight.

"Sorry, Bren, she insisted on bringing Bertie, he's okay though. Won't do nothing on yer carpet. I've brought 'er toys and some food what I know she'll eat like. She can be right fussy when she chooses. David will get 'ere as soon as he can. Told 'im not to go for a drink with his mates after training. I'd better run cos I'm late. Had to see to Mum first." She nodded at Winston, who smiled back, obviously amused by the whole scenario. She then kissed Bey on the top of her head and rushed off down the corridor.

"This is Bey, Winston. We are going to have a lovely evening together aren't we, Bey?"

The little girl was staring at Winston, her big eyes wide open, her thumb firmly wedged in her mouth. Bertie was wiggling to be set free and the lack of one retaining hand enabled him to struggle out of the blanket and land unceremoniously on the floor. He then did a circuit of Brenda's lounge/diner sniffing every few seconds at some invisible source of aroma before returning to Bey who, by now, was emptying the bag her sister had brought all over Bren's carpet. A large piece jigsaw puzzle spilled its contents and an apple rolled across the room and under the table. The rest landed in a heap of food and toys.

Winston, by now, was trying not to laugh but was obviously amused at the whole predicament that Brenda had landed herself in. "You have obviously a lot on your hands, Brenda. I would offer to help but I've got a friend coming 'round for dinner at 8 p.m. so I had better disappear. I will text you tomorrow as to how Richard is and whether they are keeping him in hospital." With that, he hastily made his retreat.

Can't blame him, thought Brenda, surveying the chaos, *I would have done the same thing at his age.* She didn't feel so bad now at not inviting him to dinner with Richard as he wouldn't have been able to come anyway.

Bey had followed Bertie under the table and was now sitting under there with the content rabbit, sitting on her lap being stroked.

"Shall we look at what Britney has brought for you, Bey? We could have a game and then I will make you some tea?"

Bey crawled out with Bertie and helped Brenda pick everything off the floor and put it on the table. There was a mini pizza, a bag of cheese and onion crisps, a carton of orange juice as well as the apple that had landed in a corner of the room.

"Bey hungry."

"Okay then, you can have your tea now. I will warm up the pizza in the microwave. You can use one of the sets of knives and forks on the table if you like," Brenda moved into the kitchen followed by Bey and Bertie, who did a circuit around the kitchen, hovering up any odd crumbs he came across, then following Bey, he went into the front room and settled down again under the table. *The nearest he could get to a burrow,* Brenda thought.

The phone rang. It was Alan. After ten minutes on the phone with him, Brenda had ascertained he had bought a new oven and hob and he couldn't get it to work. Did she have a similar one, if so could she explain to him how to get it operating? Brenda had no idea of how to solve the situation without looking at the oven herself and she could not do that as she was looking after Bey. By the time the conversation had finished, Alan was hot footing it to Brenda's flat and Brenda was turning on her oven to heat the fish and turning the hob on to cook the vegetables. She wasn't quite sure how she had managed to invite him, but she had, so she had better get on with it.

The pizza was microwaved and Bey sat at the table to eat, feeding Bertie surreptitiously under the table. She finished her crisps, took a bite of the apple and got down from the table and curled up in a ball on the settee. *No need for any of the games,* thought Brenda, *she will be sound asleep in a minute.*

Alan arrived, flourishing a bottle of wine and a box of Dairy Milk, given to him as a Christmas present from a neighbour who he did a bit of gardening for, he explained.

"Come in, Alan, it is lovely to have the company," said Brenda, who immediately regretted saying it as he might see this as a permanent invitation to dinner in the future.

"Smells nice. Is it fish?"

"Salmon, new potatoes and vegetables, followed by lemon and meringue pie."

Alan literally salivated, "Sounds delicious, Bren. I see you have worn Bey out. She's away with the fairies."

The meal went well and Brenda felt quite mellow after the large glass of wine Alan poured her. David collected Bey, who he carried down to his car in his arms, whilst Alan helped him by taking down the bag of toys.

Left on their own, Brenda and Alan talked about George, his dog bite and the predicament of his mother. They discussed Queenie and her family and the elusive Linda who Brenda had yet to meet. They even talked about Patrick, the man in the sleeping bag, that Brenda had encountered during her 'stay' in the shop after her bag had been stolen. Time flew and before they knew it, it was eleven o'clock.

"Goodness, way past my bed time," Brenda hinted.

"Yes, I must be off. I will call a taxi as I have been drinking. They are a good firm. Use them regularly. I can collect my car tomorrow before work."

The taxi dutifully arrived and Alan disappeared, thanking Brenda profusely. His oven had not been discussed, but Queenie would probably sort him out tomorrow.

Left alone at last, Brenda left the dishes in the sink, turned out the lights and got ready for bed. *Another eventful day in the life of Brenda Watts,* she thought, smiling to herself.

Chapter 21

By the time Brenda reached the shop the next day, the snow had begun to settle. Brenda's sheepskin-lined boots left black footsteps in the virgin white of the downfall. The flurry hit her face and she pulled up her scarf to protect herself. She had never been a lover of snow. Even as a child, when her mother suggested taking a tray to the top of a slope in Wellden Park and sleighing down to the bottom, she always tried to find an excuse not to go. She hated being wet and cold and saw no pleasure in the whole escapade.

Alan was already there, busy pulling a large black bin liner into the storeroom and Queenie was in the window, arranging a Christmas display. Wayne was behind the till with his earphones in, tapping his fingers on the counter as if it was a keyboard. The first thing Brenda did, was ask Queenie about George. She stopped her arrangements and got out of the window.

"He 'ad to 'ave a Tetanus injection and they bandaged his hand again and sent 'im 'ome. I took 'im back quick as I could cos of 'is mother. I offered to come in wiv him and help 'im sort 'is mother out but he wasn't having any of it. Said the carer would be wiv 'er. Ought to be in an 'ome that one. Social Services are a disgrace," she got a tissue out and blew her nose, "think I'm coming down wiv a cold. That's all I need with Christmas coming up." She climbed back into the window, "'Elp Wayne on the till will yer, Bren? It's 'is first time on."

The peace was shattered by a loud yell from the back room followed by the figure of Alan holding up a long brown furry animal, "A ferret, a bleeding, dead ferret. Who would put a ferret in a bag of clothes for a charity shop?"

"Awesome," Wayne exclaimed, "so cool. I've never seen a ferret before. Let me see him, Alan."

"Take that 'orrid, smelly thing out of the shop now, Alan. It'll put the customers off. I don't want it anywhere near me. Throw it in the bins outside. Then wash yer hands," Queenie added as an afterthought. She had clambered out of the window again and Brenda remained behind the till keeping a distance between her and the ferret. She wished Alan wouldn't dangle it in the air as it swayed like a pendulum from side to side.

Averting her eyes from the unpleasant sight, Brenda watched as a man entered the shop and taking advantage of the mayhem caused by the ferret, removed a pair of brand-new trainers from the display in the window and quickly left. Then, to Brenda's amazement, sat down on the pavement outside and removed his own shoes and had got as far as putting on the left trainer when Brenda, realising what was happening, ran out of the shop and grabbed the right trainer, brandishing it at the man. "You haven't paid for these," she shouted, "you can't just walk in and help yourself. We're not a charity." She immediately realised the irony of the sentence, as they were a charity shop.

The man looked up at her and he seemed vaguely familiar. He got up and proceeded to run and hop as fast as he could up the High Street. Queenie, Alan, Wayne and the ferret appeared at the door, watching the retreating figure.

"Patrick up to his old tricks again?" Alan commented, unaware of how strange he looked with the ferret still dangling from his hands.

"Patrick, of course, the doorway sleeper," Brenda said, remembering her sighting of him during her overnight stay in the shop.

"We let 'im 'ave a few bits and pieces now and again. He don't like that though. Prefers to nick it. He ain't very old neither. Ex-marine, I think. Saw duty in Afghanistan. Never got over it by all accounts," Queenie added, "we're not supposed to give stuff out but he's been sleeping outside our door for so long he feels like a friend. Never does anyone any 'arm. Don't know what he does through the day like, he just appears at night wiv 'is bedding and disappears before we arrive in the morning. Must 'ave seen the trainers in the winder and thought he would come back and take 'em."

"Has he not attempted to secure a council property, or, at least, sleep in a hostel?" Brenda asked.

Alan chipped in, "I asked him once when he got here and I was in the shop after we had closed, tidying 'round. He said the hostels smelled of urine and drink and you couldn't sleep in the fear of being robbed. He had his name on the list for council property but has given up. He tried to get a job then got fed up with the rejections. He held down a few security jobs for a while but he suffers with his nerves. Post Traumatic Syndrome I would guess. Fell out with his family years ago. Never married. Seems to have lost all interest in life. Sad really."

"He won't have no chance getting a council flat," Wayne added, "my uncle was on the list for years. He only got one in the end cos 'is girlfriend got pregnant. Grotty place it was as well."

Brenda thought about this, looking at the old trainers on the ground and the right trainer of the pair Patrick had taken from the window, feeling guilty that he must be hobbling about somewhere because of her. She resolved to stay behind and wait for him at the first opportunity she got, so she could match up the two trainers.

They all walked back inside hoping they had not missed any sales. The first thing Brenda noticed was a goldfish bowl on the counter and on further inspection a bag of fish food.

"Who on earth would leave a goldfish in a charity shop?"

"We can't sell any live animals, it's against the rules," Alan proclaimed, staring at the little gold fish, circling at speed around its bowl.

"I ain't never liked 'em. Won one at a fair once, gave it to me sister. It died soon after so she flushed it down the toilet," Wayne informed them.

At that moment, the door was pushed open and a small lady wrapped in a white puffer coat, woolly hat and large matching scarf and gloves entered. She looked nervous and in some pain.

"Linda!" Queenie exclaimed, "I ain't seen you in ages. You better now?"

"I'm not a hundred percent but my doctor said I ought to get out of the house. I find the buses hard to get on nowadays with my hip so I got a taxi. Lovely young man helped me in and out of it. I would have rung but I knew it was my usual day to volunteer so I have just come down instead. Don't worry if you don't need me. I can always go to the library and get a Mills and Boon out. I've nearly finished the one I am reading at the moment."

"We can always use another pair of 'ands," Queenie replied, "you ain't met our Bren yet or Wayne. Bren's 'ere every day and Wayne's on Work Experience."

"Nice to meet you both. I have had one thing after another since the summer, never quite well enough to come in. I missed the shop though. Probably forgotten how to use the till."

There was a chorus of reassurances and Linda's coat and bag were taken into the back room, a cup of tea was made for her and a chair brought out so she could sit behind the till when not serving. It struck Brenda just how kind everyone was and how lucky she was to have been able to get to know them all.

While this was all going on, two customers had asked Wayne about the goldfish and been told it wasn't for sale. He was about to take it through to the back when Linda uttered a cry of approval. "He is just like my Goldie. I miss him circling around his bowl. Company for me really even though he couldn't be hugged or taken for a walk. I've always loved fish ever since I won one in Southend at a fair."

"You're welcome to 'ave 'im, Linda. We're not allowed to sell fish, so he is all yours."

Linda looked pleased and followed Wayne to the till, "I don't know how I will get him home, Wayne, not on a bus with my dodgy hip." Brenda just about heard Wayne offering to 'elp her and also the familiar ring tone of her mobile phone.

"I'd better answer that, you never know it could be urgent."

Brenda dug her phone out of her bag. There was a voice message on it. It was Winston. Richard was back at home but could Brenda pop in on her way back from work as he was on duty. He sounded concerned. Brenda tried to ring him back but the phone had been turned off.

She made a mental note to call in on Richard. Perhaps she could leave a little bit early, especially as Linda was here now as well. Wayne carried the goldfish into the back room before returning to the till. Brenda, saw they were both on the till so she started to tidy up the rails, getting all the clothes colour coordinated and the right sizes together. Queenie returned to the Christmas Window Display, humming to herself and wearing a Father Christmas hat, wedged down over her perm. Queenie obviously loved Christmas, Brenda hadn't enjoyed a Christmas for years. The day had only meant a cold feeling of being alone when everyone else was surrounded by family. Would it be different this year? She certainly knew more people, but they would be busy with their own families and she would never intrude on those arrangements, even if anyone was kind enough to ask her. She had wondered about volunteering, at the churches who fed the homeless their Christmas Dinner, but had never got around to it, since she had been working in the Charity Shop though she had more confidence and would feel able to do it now. She would look into it.

Queenie told her to leave at three to enable her to get around to Richard's flat at about 3:30 p.m. She was even able to pick up a newspaper for him and a four pack of Guinness, a drink she remembered he liked.

It was very cold and the Christmas lights were being erected in the High Street. Brenda wondered when the

'Lighting Up' ceremony would be. She usually went to this, looking around all the food and bric-a-brac stalls. She had never really had anyone to buy a present for after her mother died. She had bought the newspaper girl a little something last year. She always felt sorry for the kids who did these early morning rounds. Brenda had once asked her mother if she could do one when she was very young but her mother said she wasn't having a daughter of hers wandering the streets at some ungodly hour poking papers through doors. Also, she could be bitten by some vicious dog waiting for her in the semi-dark. So that had been the end of that. Instead, Brenda got a Saturday job in Woolworths on the biscuit counter. She remembered selling broken biscuits, crumbs everywhere, mouse traps under the counters. *Long gone are those days*, *as well as Woolworths itself.* Ruminating on this and feeling quite reminiscent, Brenda made her way back home.

Chapter 22

At first, there was no reply to her ringing Richard's doorbell and she wondered if he had gone out. Then the door opened a crack and Richard's head poked out of the space, "Oh, Brenda, I wondered who it was." He looked tired and confused. There was a plaster on his forehead and he had black eyes that gave him a panda look.

"I just thought I would pop in and see how you were. Winston said you'd had a fall. It is so slippery, underfoot, I am wearing my walking boots to work on some days."

Richard still looked a bit blank.

"Is there anything I can get you?" Brenda remembered her gifts and presented them to Richard, "I thought these might cheer you up." Richard took the carrier bag off Brenda but did not look inside it.

"The funeral for Maureen. It is next Friday. I must organise a wake and inform people. You were good enough to go through the telephone book with me. I wondered…"

"Of course, I will, Richard, why don't I do it now. I will make a note of the addresses and send letters to them. We can order some sandwich platters and a couple of quiches. It is all people want with a cup of tea or coffee."

Richard stepped aside to let her in, looking relieved that someone was taking over, "Winston has booked the crematorium for 11 a.m. and the hearse and cars. He has been very good to me. I must remember to buy him something when the funeral is over."

"I am sure he does not expect anything, Richard. He is just a very good person. He isn't looking for a reward."

Brenda and Richard made a list of the names of friends they thought would like to pay their respects and Brenda was

155

about to leave when she remembered their previous dinner arrangement. "Richard, you had your fall on the night you were coming to dinner with me. I wondered if you would like to come to me on Saturday instead."

Richard paused for a moment, probably still feeling guilty to be doing any socialising so soon after the death of Maureen, "That would be very nice, I will bring a bottle of wine. Seven o'clock was it?"

Brenda returned to her flat, making a mental note to inform Winston of the plans. She would shop tomorrow as officially this was her day off. She would check with George first to see if they had enough staff. Friday was a busy day.

She was about to make her calls when there was a light tap on her door. She thought it might be Winston. On opening the door, she was met with the smiling face of Bey. In her hands was a parcel wrapped in Christmas paper, swathed in Sellotape and a card precariously balanced on top, "'appy Cwistmas Bwen."

Brenda was stunned into silence. She felt tears welling. Never had she been so thrilled to receive a present. She bent down and hugged the tiny form just as Britney appeared around the corner where she had obviously been hiding, "She wanted to give you your present on 'er own. I know it's early, like, but she was too excited about it to wait to nearer Christmas day. I 'ope you like it."

"I will love it whatever it is. Come in, come in, I will get you a drink and open my present."

Brenda ushered them both in, took their coats and sat them down whilst she put the kettle on and poured some juice for Bey. When she returned to the room, Bey was whispering in Britney's ear.

"She ses yer not allowed to open the present until Christmas day cos Father Christmas will tell yer off," Britney smiled at Brenda who was amazed that children still believed in Father Christmas in these days of technology. It was quite a comforting thought that children could still be children in some areas of life.

"You are right, Bey, I will put it somewhere very safe. I haven't got yours yet as I want it to be very special, something you really want."

Bey looked up at Bren and then her sister and took a deep breath before uttering a long "meow" and then hiding behind Britney's chair, giggling. Brenda assumed this was some kind of game and laughed with her. "Meow, meow," the little girl continued, jumping up and down on the spot until Britney got up and scooped her into her arms.

"Stop it, Bey, or Father Christmas ain't going to buy you anyfing."

"Bey want Meow," this time she directed her plea at Bren who had caught on what it was all about.

"You want a cat for Christmas?"

"She ain't having no cat, Bren. Me ma would go spare. We've got a dog a rabbit and there are six kids in the 'ouse. Me Ma is never well so she ain't going to be very 'appy if another animal appears. Too much 'ard work."

Brenda considered this problem, "I am not allowed any pets living here with me, Bey, as the man who owns the flats does not allow them. I would love a dog or a cat but I have to accept I won't have one unless I move into a house and then I can have what I want. I think you are so lucky having Max and Bertie."

Bey was obviously thinking about this, clinging to her sister, her head buried in Britney's neck. Just at that moment, there was a ring at the door. Brenda answered it and there was Winston, smiling and looking less fraught than previously.

"Hi, Brenda, just thought I would pop by and see how things were going. Richard says you are organising the invites and the catering for the wake?"

"Come in, Britney and Bey have just popped by. I've got the kettle on."

"No, I won't come in, I must get to the shops. I have been on a double-shift today. Just wondered when we could meet up and talk about the arrangements?"

"Can you come to dinner tonight? Richard is coming around at seven? Nothing posh, just something I can cobble together."

"That would be just fine, Brenda. I will see you then. I'll bring a bottle of wine." With that, he disappeared up the corridor. *Two men and two bottles of wine*, Brenda thought. Things were really looking up. She returned to Britney and Bey, who seemed to have forgotten about the cat.

Instead, she was pointing at the settee, "Spidey, spidey, spidey." The mantra was endless. Brenda could see a black 'thing' partially hidden with a cushion. It was the one thing Brenda hated – Spiders. However, she had learnt this over the years and had a litter picker she used for such occasions as she couldn't bear to touch the horrible creatures. She rushed into the kitchen to retrieve it and back again to the settee. Carefully, so as not to frighten it into running and hiding elsewhere, she aimed the litter picker at the spider with the intention of lifting it up and depositing it outside the door. The spider was particularly still and Brenda wondered if it was dead. She picked it up with the pickers – it was hard, it was plastic! Bey and Britney burst into laughter.

"Sorry, Bren. She plays that trick on everyone. 'Ope you wasn't frightened?"

Brenda was aware of how ridiculous she must look trying to gather up a plastic spider with a litter picker. It brought back bad memories of being bullied and teased at school which then carried on into the workplace. However, this was different, this was a small child playing a harmless prank on her. This was the ideal opportunity to cast away all those feelings of being persecuted and embrace her new life and her new friends. So instead of being hurt, she burst into laughter, accompanied by Britney and Bey.

Then Britney went silent, it was obvious she wanted to say something but was finding it difficult. "Bren, I got into the college course, start next term. Gor a problem though. One of the lectures is in the evening and me ma has just gor 'erself a cleaning job and none of the boys will look after Bey. It's only for a couple of hours like on a Friday. I will come straight back. She likes you and I feel 'appy she is with you cos I trust you. Ma will pay you, like," she added.

Brenda was taken aback. Voluntary worker and now childminder. "I would feel insulted to be paid, Britney. It would be a pleasure to look after Bey. We get on really well, don't we, Bey?" The little girl nodded. "As long as there are no more spiders," Brenda added, ruffling Bey's hair.

"Cheers, Bren, come on, Bey, better get going," mission accomplished, Britney gathered Bey and her belongings up and headed for the door. Then, she stopped, returned to Brenda and unselfconsciously put her arms around her and gave her a hug. Brenda was taken aback by this show of emotion and hugged her back. These two girls were now like the family she had never had. She felt quite tearful but pulled herself together.

"I will text you, Britney, so we can meet before Christmas and I can give you your Christmas presents. Let me know if you can think of anything Bey would like, besides a cat." Brenda felt a thrill at having someone she loved to buy for. Christmas would mean something this year.

Chapter 23

Friday morning Brenda rang George's mobile phone to ask him if it was all right to have the day off so she could shop and do her neglected housework in preparation for the dinner party she had arranged with Richard and Winston. The phone remained unanswered so Brenda left a long message, hoping he would pick it up and ring her back. She rang Alan next who said George had taken his mother for an assessment with the Social Services and they were trying to find a suitable care home for her. Brenda was glad that some action was at last being sought for his mother. Perhaps now George would be less stressed. The bad news was that Linda had taken a turn for the worse and would not be in tomorrow and Queenie was going with George to look at some homes, so there would only be Wayne and himself to 'man' the shop. Could she possibly help out? Brenda had no choice, this was definitely becoming a full-time vocational commitment, and, actually, Brenda felt quite *comfortable* with that.